CONCEALED IDENTITY

JESSICA R. PATCH

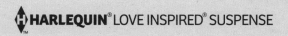

HARLEQUIN® LOVE INSPIRED® SUSPENSE

LOVE INSPIRED BOOKS

Recycling programs for this product may not exist in your area.

ISBN-13: 978-0-373-45685-7

Concealed Identity

www.Harlequin.com

Printed in U.S.A.

"Blair, you're in trouble. I can tell."

She wouldn't look him in the eye.

"Fine. Don't tell me." Frustration leaped into his words. Not just because he was losing precious time finding her brother and his colleague, but he wanted her trust. Holt wanted her to lean on him.

Even though he shouldn't.

"I—"

"It's obvious you're worried but you won't go to the police." He softened. It was time to give her the peace she so desperately needed. "I know someone who can help who isn't a cop. He's a private investigator. And he could look into what happened. Maybe find out where Jeremy is."

For a brief moment her chin quivered and her eyes seemed hopeful, but she tamped it down. Inhaling deeply, she shook her head. "Jeremy has a friend. Someone he said he could depend on. He helped him get clean and keeps him accountable. He might know where Jeremy is. Could you...could you help me find him?"

Holt's insides wilted.

Yeah. He could help her find that friend. She was staring right at him with watery eyes, and he wanted desperately to tell her. His gut said she was innocent. But his job said to follow protocol. He'd never been more torn. But he'd never once broken cover. He couldn't start now.

Jessica R. Patch lives in the mid-South, where she pens inspirational contemporary romance and romantic suspense novels. When she's not hunched over her laptop or going on adventurous trips with willing friends in the name of research, you can find her watching way too much Netflix with her family and collecting recipes to amazing dishes she'll probably never cook. To learn more about Jessica, please visit her at jessicarpatch.com.

Books by Jessica R. Patch

Love Inspired Suspense

Fatal Reunion
Protective Duty
Concealed Identity

Now hope does not disappoint,
because the love of God has been poured out
in our hearts by the Holy Spirit who was given to us.
–Romans 5:5

To my son, Myles, for inspiring me with your endless imagination and amazing me with your servant's heart. I love you.

Thanks go out to:

My agent, Rachel Kent, for continuing to champion and believe in my writing.

My editor, Shana Asaro. As always, thank you for your keen eye and amazing editorial skills.

Susan Tuttle: thank you for brainstorming and seeing me through yet another book.

Special thanks to Sergeant/SWAT Commander Greg Carson for helping me get my DEA information correct and for so many great ideas. If something's *not* right, or stretched, it's my fault!

And to Jesus. For Your glory always. My hope is in You alone.

ONE

Blair Sullivan glanced in the side-view mirror of her company's box truck. The dark SUV seemed a little too close for comfort, and with her past, she wasn't taking any chances. Not when the windows were tinted far beyond the legal limit. It looked exactly like the types of vehicles she'd ridden in over the years.

And no one good had ever been inside.

Pulse skittering, she laid on the gas while her sister, Gigi, obliviously switched radio stations and rambled about lunch destination choices. She must have pressed the pause button with her on-again, off-again boyfriend who co-owned the Black-Eyed Pea. That was where they normally ate their meals, since neither had mastered the kitchen, unless peanut butter and jelly counted.

"It's hotter than blue blazes." Gigi lifted her hair, a shade lighter and a few inches shorter than Blair's, from her neck. "You notice Mr. Hollywood noticing you at the auction this morning? Because I did. I also noticed you noticing him."

Could she use *notice* in a sentence one more time?

Blair's stomach roiled as she glanced in her side-view mirror again. The SUV continued to follow. Could be paranoia. She'd been looking over her shoulder since her late husband, Mateo, was gunned down in Colombia. Not long after their wedding, she'd discovered he was a drug lord in a major cartel and not the man she'd believed him to be. But at that point, it was too late to get out alive. Blair had shielded Gigi from that world of fear, and she wasn't about to pull her into it now.

It's a casual drive home. Act normal.

A few cars sped by. Not much traffic this Saturday morning. Her heart rate continued to elevate as memories surfaced, but she forced herself to engage in conversation. "He wasn't noticing me. He was watching to see if I'd keep bidding on the storage unit." He had been attractive, though. Built like a superhero made of steel. Dark scruff that did little to hide the deep dimple in his squared chin.

Okay, so she'd noticed. Every woman at the storage unit auction had perked up when he had swaggered onto the scene. Not just because he was movie star good-looking, but he was new to the monthly auctions. "That reminds me, did you see Ronnie Lawson or hear him mention he wouldn't be there today?"

The SUV continued to ride her bumper. She was going seventy!

"How does Mr. Hollywood even remotely remind you of Ronnie?" She snorted. "I didn't hear jack, but I know you'd have lost that unit if he had. He seems to enjoy out-bidding you." Gigi paused, her dark eyes concerned. "Hey, you okay? You look wigged out."

Blair cleared her throat. "I'm fine." She breathed evenly, pasted a fake smile on her face and hammered the gas pedal as she exited the ramp onto the outskirts of her small town of Hope, Tennessee. The place where she'd started over. Where her grandparents had lived most of their lives. The only place Blair had ever felt safe and at home. "Just feeling buyer's remorse. I may have paid more than I should for that unit."

She'd hoped the SUV wouldn't have taken the ramp, too. But it had. *What to do... What to do...*

"You'll know once you get home and inventory everything. So, about the guy. He looked exactly like Superman. Coal-black hair. And those eyes. No one has eyes that blue but Superman."

At twenty-six, and two years younger than Blair, Gigi acted more like fifteen. She wasn't going to let up on the hot topic. Mystery Auction Man was no Superman. Superman didn't hold wildfire in his eyes. Red flags had flown high. She'd been duped by charm and good looks before and ended up marrying the man behind them. Never again. No more falling for liars and men who pretended to be one thing when they were something else entirely.

Blair changed lanes, the SUV stayed in the right one. Okay, maybe she was being paranoid after all. A few cars zinged by, leaving the bypass she was now on empty. Only them and the SUV.

"Fine," Gigi said, "if you don't want to talk about Mr. Hollywood, let's talk about our brother. You heard from him?"

Another flop of her stomach. Jeremy hadn't called or answered any of her texts and voice mails in several days. It wasn't like she could pop on over to his apartment, since he lived in Memphis, though she'd tried to get him to move to Hope. Closer to her and Gigi since their father traveled regularly now that he was retired. Right now he was off in the West Indies and her brother was AWOL. Surely Jeremy hadn't relapsed. He'd been doing so well. *Lord, please keep Jeremy out of trouble again. Watch over him.*

The SUV changed lanes and zoned in on her bumper. Blair white-knuckled the steering wheel and slid her upper lip into her mouth, concentrating. Thinking. Praying. *Lord, let me simply be paranoid.* She shifted back into the right lane, hoping the driver was in a hurry and would pass her.

Please. Please. Please.

Pulse pounding as they shifted in behind her, Blair inhaled and exhaled. "Can you turn the radio down?" She couldn't think straight. Her head buzzed.

"Why?" Gigi lowered the volume but huffed. "Blair, what's wrong with you?"

The SUV rammed the back of her truck.

Gigi squealed. "What was that?"

"Sit tight." Blair increased speed. Nothing but fields for miles on their way home. Of course, she wasn't dumb enough to try to make it there and lead her pursuer to the house, but she didn't know where to go or what to do. She could hardly swallow.

She glanced in the rearview.

The SUV was gone!

But there it was in her side mirror, gaining.

"Reach under the seat and get my gun, Gigi!"

"Gun! You carry a gun?" Gigi's eyes widened, hysteria and questions blaring loud and clear.

Blair didn't have a choice. "Now is not the time. Get it," she hollered, and floored it. Gigi's hands trembled as she handed Blair her Glock.

"What are you going to do?" Gigi's voice squeaked with panic.

Good question. She had to protect Gigi and herself. Blair had learned a thing or two—if only indirectly—being married to Mateo. Always be wary and always be on the offense.

She rolled her window down and aimed the gun, hoping her time at the gun range and some prayer would help her hit the tire and spin the SUV out.

Gigi's anxious cries echoed through the cab.

Blair gripped the gun with clammy hands, lungs squeezing, and fired a round.

The SUV rammed her again, sending them lurching. What was that thing made of—steel? The passenger window lowered. A man she didn't recognize, wearing dark glasses, raised the barrel of a gun.

Blair cracked off another shot, missing the tire, but hitting the metal around it. The SUV swerved, giving them time to veer ahead.

Gigi screeched.

Cracks sounded in the body of the truck.

"Lord, save us!" Blair prayed, then shifted in her seat. "Take the wheel and the gas!" she commanded, and raised her gun, firing at the tires again. Blood whooshed in her ears, and her throat had turned as dry as dead grass.

Gigi scooted over, gathered the wheel and replaced Blair's foot with hers on the gas pedal. "I'm scared!"

"Me, too, G. Hold on and pray." Blair didn't want to hang out the window, but she couldn't get a clear shot at the tire. What other choice was there? If she didn't spin the SUV out, she and Gigi might get killed.

Blair turned in the driver's seat and leaned out the window.

Another pop pierced the air, and the SUV struck the corner edge of her vehicle.

"I'm losing control," Gigi shrieked, and flinched. "Blair!"

Her truck swerved and Blair whirled around to take the wheel, but it was too late. They sailed into the ditch on the right side of the road.

Shots were fired in rapid succession as if a gun war was happening behind them.

Blair's head nailed the steering wheel. Her neck popped and a blinding pain shot clear to her toes. Gigi, eyes closed, slumped against the passenger-side door, her long walnut hair covering her face.

"Gigi!" Blair called.

Another round of shots were fired.

With blurred vision, she groped for the gun that had clattered to the floorboard and grabbed it. She had to save them from whoever was trying to kill them. Why were they being targeted?

Blair forced the driver's door open. Hot, sticky blood oozed down her forehead and cheek. Hands shaking, she stumbled into the brush on the side of the road. The world tipped.

The SUV fled the scene as a red truck stopped on the side of the road.

A man bounded toward her as she tottered to the ground.

DEA Agent Holt McKnight raced toward the woman he'd identified as Blair Sullivan, who had collapsed into the waist-high weeds. He'd been on his way back from the auction outside town but had to stop about six miles back for gas. Somewhere between the gas station and here, someone had emerged and tried—worst-case scenario—to kill Blair and her sister. Best-case, scare and run them off the road.

Based on things her brother, Jeremy, had told Holt in casual conversations, Blair wouldn't hurt a fly. From the hailstorm of bullets, Holt wasn't so sure. Not exactly the same innocent-looking woman he'd observed at the storage auction this morning.

Either way, Holt had a job to do and Blair Sullivan's sunny smile and warm eyes weren't going to interfere. Jeremy, his criminal informant, and Bryan Livingston, his DEA colleague, were missing. The only connection between the disappearances was Alejandro Gonzalez, the right-hand man of the Juarez Mexican Cartel, who had last been seen in Hope.

Holt had jumped on the undercover assignment to investigate and hopefully find Agent Livingston and Jeremy alive. He'd never forgive himself if something happened to Jeremy. Not only was he his CI, but Holt had been mentoring him over a year after helping him get into rehab in Memphis.

Holt knelt over Blair. Blood slicked her cheek and neck, but the injury didn't appear too bad. Next to her lay a Glock .380 auto. Slimline. Nice choice. It appeared Blair knew guns. But then, she'd been married to a criminal who trafficked them along with drugs. How could a woman who seemed so kind and gentle have gotten messed up with someone like Mateo Salvador?

Holt checked her pulse. Steady.

Blair's long eyelashes fluttered and rose to reveal dazed eyes the color of medium-roasted coffee beans. Man, but she was beautiful. *Get a grip, Holt. She's a person of interest and you know her past.* She shot up and skittered back. "Get away from me!" She searched along the ground frantically.

Holt raised her gun. "Looking for this?"

Terror pulsed in her eyes, and she held her hands up. "I don't want any trouble."

"Then that makes two of us." But trouble had reared its ugly head. Question was, had it come for her or because of her?

Easing into his cover, he pasted on a grin, hoping to disarm her. He needed Blair Sullivan to trust him. "I'm Holt Renard. Was on my way home when I came up behind that vehicle." He'd been following her for two days, not that he wouldn't recognize her. Jeremy had a few family photos on his mantel, and Holt had thoroughly examined the case files on Mateo Salvador. "Why were they shooting at you?"

Not that she'd tell him if she did know, but she was scared and it might tumble out. Had it been Alejandro in that SUV? Or Hector Salvador, her late husband's brother and the head of the Colombian Salvador Cartel? Did he find out Blair was fraternizing with his greatest enemy? Was she playing both sides? Eyes that held goodness and honesty told him she wasn't playing anyone. But looks could be deceiving.

Recognition lit her face. "I know you. You were at the auction today. Trying to outbid me. You're Superman."

Wow, she'd really nailed her head good. He'd been called a lot of things, but Superman wasn't one of them. Had to admit, he kinda liked the idea. But reality smacked him with truth. Holt was no one's hero. The one person he'd wanted to save most in his life, he couldn't.

He cocked his head and contained his amusement.

She shook her head as if confused. "Did I say that out loud?"

"That I'm Superman? Yeah. You said that. And you're right—I was at the auction today." It had been a great place to blend in and study her without raising suspicion. He didn't think she'd paid him a lick of attention. Apparently, she had. He clasped her hands and helped her to her feet. She swayed a bit, and he steadied her. "Got a name?" he asked.

"Gigi!" Blair's face flashed with panic, and she hobbled to her truck. She opened the passenger door, and Blair's sister moaned and touched her head as she exited the vehicle. A small cut above her forehead oozed a few drops of blood. "You okay, G?"

Gigi nodded and then threw up in the field.

"We need to get her to a hospital." Holt stepped closer. Blair held Gigi's hair away from her face and soothed her, stroking her back. Holt's chest squeezed. Her soft voice and words of comfort to her sister moved him, not to mention she was ridiculously pretty. Fairly tall, even compared to his six-foot-three frame. Curvy where she should be, but delicate. Surely this woman wasn't neck-deep in drug trafficking.

Gigi turned in his direction and moaned. "Naturally, the guy with the eyes would see me ralph."

Holt chuckled. "If it makes you feel any better, you did it gracefully."

"It doesn't."

Blair smirked, then sobered. "I want to get out of here." She looked at Holt. "Blair. Sullivan. And this is my sister—"

"Gigi. Yeah I got that. Seems you might need a little medical attention." He pointed to her head.

She touched it and sighed. "It's not that bad. Thank you for checking on us."

Not that Holt came to their aid to get close to Blair, but he did hope it might be an open door to gain her confidence. Whether she was involved with the cartel or not, Blair could be the key to helping him find Jeremy and Bryan. And time was not on his side.

"What happened? Who were those crazies?" Gigi took the water bottle Blair gave her and swished some water in her mouth before spitting it out and climbing back inside the truck.

"Yeah, who were those crazies?" Holt asked, frowning. Blair had no business driving after knocking her head like that.

Blair shrugged. "I don't know, but I'm not sticking around in case they decide to come back and introduce themselves. Thanks again for your help."

"Yeah, thanks, Mr. Hollywood." Gigi smiled and then winced.

"It's Holt, in case the head injury has you confused."
With all the acting he was about to do, Hollywood fit
much better than Superman.

Blair leaned out her driver's-side window. She looked
too petite to be driving this bulky thing. But clearly, the
woman was strong. And brave. "Had you not shown up
when you did, I don't know what would have happened.
You must have scared them off."

Holt studied her, searching her eyes for answers to what
might have actually gone wrong. Nothing there but terror
and confusion. "I guess I did." It took squeezing off a few
rounds himself. Relieved Blair didn't realize he'd used his
weapon, he relaxed his shoulders. "You sure you're okay
to drive? I can give you a lift to the hospital, and we can
come back for your truck later."

Blair's face blanched.

Did she not plan on seeking medical attention? Not if
she didn't want questions raised.

"I can manage," Blair finally said. "Besides, my stuff's
in the back and I'm not leaving it." She narrowed her eyes.
"We'll be fine."

Holt couldn't blame Blair for being suspicious of him,
but he'd have to remedy it. Quick. If saving her life didn't
get him in her good graces, he wasn't sure what would.
Charm? He could lay that on pretty thick when necessary, but something about the way she'd carried herself
and avoided eye contact with him at the storage auction
said charm wasn't the way to go to win her trust.

Honesty might be the ticket. But that was one thing
he couldn't give. Came with the territory. "You sure?"

"Positive. Thanks again." That was her polite Southern
belle dismissal.

"Okay." He ambled toward his truck with no intention
of letting them out of his sight. Blair cranked the engine
and it sputtered to life. She pulled through the tall grass

and back onto the road from the shallow ditch. Holt followed at a distance, hoping not to further scare them, but this was the only way into town, and he wanted to make sure they were safe.

As he suspected, they went straight to their home. No medical attention. He clambered out of his truck.

"Why are you following us?" Blair demanded.

He held his hands up in surrender. "You took a whack to the head. Just wanted to make sure you got safely home."

"Well, we did."

Holt turned to Gigi, who was tottering out of the truck. He rushed to help her. "How do you feel?"

"Like I got hit by a truck."

Holt winked. "Imagine that. Are you not going to the hospital? You really should."

Blair came around and slipped in between Holt and Gigi, creating a protective barrier. "I can take it from here." She shifted her eyes toward Gigi and studied her sister's face, as if she were in a battle about whether she should go or not.

"I feel woozy, Blair."

Blair sighed. "We'll go see Doc Drummond."

Ah. The local doctor. "What about the police?" he asked. Didn't matter to him as much as them receiving some medical care. Better if she didn't call the police. They'd only get in his way. Besides, based on the homework he'd done on the town, the sheriff was recovering at home from a stroke and the deputy chief was in charge. He was only a year younger than Holt's thirty-two years. Probably didn't know diddly-squat. This town barely had two thousand residents. Biggest crime might be cow tipping.

Then again, Alejandro Gonzalez had been spotted here by Agent Livingston, so who knew what was going on? A place like this wouldn't be on anyone's radar. Could Alejandro have been meeting the head of the Juarez Cartel? No one had ever seen his face before. Which meant he could be hiding right under their noses.

Did Blair know who he was? Was that why she'd moved here after her husband had been gunned down by the Juarez Cartel? Had she been in on Mateo's execution? Or had the head of the snake moved here to lie in wait and strike at Blair as a move against her former brother-in-law, Hector Salvador?

Too many questions clogging the wheel. Holt inhaled and exhaled, concentrating on the here and now.

"I'll call the police once I get my sister to Doc Drummond's." Her tone didn't sound convincing, and her eyes shifted before she looked away. Nope. She wasn't calling anyone. Seemed odd for someone innocent. "Let me drive you. I know you managed to drive home, but neither of you seem to be in any shape to be behind a wheel." It killed Holt to see a hurting woman. A stray thought of his high school love crashed into his mind. She'd hurt for so long before the cancer took her, ruining all their dreams for a future together.

But he didn't want to think about it. Thinking meant feeling. And Holt didn't want to feel. Not even right now while looking at the lovely Blair Sullivan. He was feeling something. Something he shouldn't. She was an assignment. That was all.

Blair gnawed her bottom lip. "I think we'll be okay."

Gigi was already walking toward his truck. "Do you know where Doc Drummond's office is?"

"I just moved here, but it's a small town. In fact, it appears you and I are neighbors. I rented the McCowens' house across the street."

"Cool." Gigi climbed inside the Ford F-150 he was

using as his cover vehicle. "You have a head injury, Blair. I don't want to wreck for the second time today. So get in."

Blair hesitated and chewed on her thumbnail as if considering the offer. "So you live across the street." She eyed him. "What brings you to Hope?"

"I'm opening up a used outdoorsman store. Kind of a dream of mine. That's why I was at the auction today. Trying to stock the place." And the lies continued. Worst part of his job—especially if he was lying to someone innocent. He wasn't sure she was, but he wanted her to be.

Blair scowled at Gigi, who had taken up homestead in his truck. "And where is your business?"

Okay, this might be a little too coincidental, but he'd make it work. "Only place I could find for the right price. I leased a building on the square. Right by what appears to be your shop." He pointed to her bulky box truck. The side was painted with a huge Christmas tree, and the name of her business was scrolled in red: It's A Wonderful Life Antiques. "Guess we'll be seeing a lot of each other, neighbor."

Blair didn't budge. She wasn't buying it. The woman was tough. Smart. If she wasn't a person of interest professionally, he'd admit she was definitely someone he'd like to get to know personally. But nothing serious. Holt's heart couldn't afford to do serious.

"Don't worry, I won't come knocking for a cup of sugar. I don't bake." If Holt could put her at ease, lower her guard, he could get close. At this rate, he wasn't getting nearer than arm's length, and that wasn't good enough.

"Neither does she," Gigi called from the cab of the truck. "My head hurts. Let's go."

Blair stepped forward and froze. "My gun! Where's my gun?"

"I have it. You weren't exactly thinking clearly back there."

"I'd like it back before I go anywhere with you." Her tone was laced with suspicion, caution.

Holt slipped it from his waistband and handed it to her. "What are you doing carrying a gun?"

"Why does anyone carry a gun? And I live in the South." She grabbed her purse from her truck, tucked her gun inside, locked the doors and slowly made her way to his truck. He hoped she had a license to carry a concealed weapon. "Gigi, get out. I'll take the middle."

Safeguarding her little sister from the mysterious and probably—in Blair's eyes—dangerous man. Something about her fierce protectiveness unraveled a cord he'd kept a tight rein over.

No doubt, this woman would sacrifice herself for her family. Whether she was the good guy or the bad. But which was she?

Blair sat next to Holt in Doc Drummond's office, staring through the gold lettering painted across the large picture window announcing that this was indeed a doctor's office. The heat filtering through the pane warmed her face.

"You doing all right?" Holt asked. He hadn't budged since they entered. This man didn't even know them. Why would he stick around like this?

"What do you think?" She hadn't meant the question to come with a sting. "Sorry." Blair lightly touched the bandaged area of her head where she'd hit it against the steering wheel. Thankfully, her hair covered it. She didn't need the town asking a bunch of questions, although news traveled at warp speed, so they'd know about the wreck. Not the bullets, though. And she preferred to keep it that way.

Doc Drummond had bought her quick story, which wasn't a lie, of losing control of the wheel and running off Farley Pass. She probably should have come here in the first place, but she'd been rattled and frightened. She'd wanted to get home. Safe.

Down the cobbled streets, neighbors bounced in and out of shops. Kids licked dripping ice-cream cones; friends laughed and peeked inside each other's shopping bags. Vehicles lined the area in front of the regal courthouse.

Felicity Potts, the owner of Read It and Steep Bookstore and Tea Company, was sweeping the welcome mat. Blair caught her eye and she waved.

Blair waved back.

"Tea shop. How about I go over there and get a cup for you?" Holt asked.

Blair tried to see past Holt's good looks to the kindness he showed. Was it real? When it came to men, her judgment stank. Mateo had proven that. "Are you going to get some for yourself, too?"

"Yeah, I don't do tea."

Blair smirked; couldn't help it. "Chamomile." She reached into her purse. "Let me get you some cash."

He laid a hand over hers. "I got it. Be back in a minute."

"Thank you. For the fourth time."

"Five if you want to thank me for the drive over." He swept his dark hair out of his eyes and left, jogging across the street.

Blair loved Felicity's tea. She loved this town. Barely any crime. But today someone had tried to kill Blair and Gigi. Guilt wound her shoulders tight and drummed in her neck. She'd brought a can of worms to Hope. Somehow. Holt had asked her if she was going to call the police. It had almost sounded like he was testing her. Could the man buying her a chamomile tea be behind the attack? His popping up seemed awfully suspicious, but he'd done nothing but help and be friendly.

Mateo had been friendly, too. Charming. Sweet. Fun. Look where that had gotten her.

She leaned her head against the glass and closed her eyes.

The door opened and a blast of heat sucked the cool air from the waiting area. "Blair Sullivan. What in the world happened to your head?"

Blair didn't need to look up to know who was standing over her. The familiar sugary scent permeated the room as her voice tinkled. Riella Drummond. Doc's wife. "G and I had a car accident on the way home from the auction today." Blair opened her eyes to the most-well-put-together woman she'd ever seen. Hair worthy of shampoo commercials and naturally bronzed skin.

Riella sat next to her and laid her purse on a table filled with up-to-date magazines. "Do you need anything? I can have Sophia bring dinner over."

Sophia, Riella's housekeeper, made a mean enchilada dish, but Blair didn't feel right about taking something for nothing, especially when nobody was dying. "No need for all the fuss. We'll grab a bite at the Black-Eyed Pea if G feels up to it."

"Ah. Well, I just came to bring my man something to eat. He missed lunch. You sure you don't want anything? I have plenty."

Blair inhaled the tangy scent of Italian food. She must have stopped in at Mangiare. Another reason Blair adored this town—the wide variety of ethnic groups represented here. And the variety of food choices because of it. It really was a wonderful life.

Until today.

"No, really. I'm fine and Gigi will need to get home soon anyway. She'll probably want to lie down."

Riella glanced outside. "You met the man who leased the store next to yours yet?"

Holt Renard. "I did. He gave us a lift, but I don't really know much about him." Not nearly enough to feel comfortable. And with the way he'd sent her pulse skittering at the auction, she couldn't get to know him. "He's opening an outdoorsman store."

Riella's eyebrow lifted. "Speaking of..."

Holt made an entrance and handed Blair her tea.

Riella introduced herself and chitchatted with Holt while Blair sipped her chamomile tea and fretted. She hoped he wouldn't blab to Riella about the circumstances surrounding the wreck. But Blair couldn't tell him not to, either. She'd instructed Gigi to keep mum before she saw Doc. She'd have to do some explaining when she got her alone. She'd never wanted Gigi to know how stupid and naive she'd been to fall in with Mateo and his crowd. No way around it now.

"Well, on behalf of Hope, welcome. I'll have Sophia whip you up a welcome meal."

Riella didn't mind offering meals to everyone and anyone. She never had to cook them.

Doc Drummond led Gigi into the waiting area. "No concussion, but watch her anyway. She can take Motrin for the pain. Wake her up every thirty minutes to an hour just in case, and she'll be right as rain." He flashed a grin at his wife. "I smell a meatball sub."

Riella raised a red-and-green bag. "You're welcome." She kissed his cheek. Blair hooked her arm around Gigi's. "Thanks, Doc. We appreciate your help."

"Be more careful next time, Blair. That beast of a truck is a lot to handle." Doc Drummond winked. "Nice meeting you, Holt. I'll have to swing by and check out the store when it's up and running."

"Sounds good."

Doc escorted his wife to the offices. Holt held the door while Blair and Gigi stepped outside underneath the white-and-yellow awning. Even with the shade, it felt like they were charging toward a fire-breathing dragon.

Blair looked at Holt. "Can I have a couple of minutes alone with my sister?"

"Sure." Holt paused, then meandered down the sidewalk out of earshot.

Blair turned to Gigi. "I guess you kept quiet about what really happened."

"You told me not to say a word, so I listened. I'm not sure what did happen. Are you?"

"Let's talk about it later. Are you hungry?" Blair studied Gigi. Her color had come back, but her eyes looked tired. And scared.

"I feel like talking about it now. Why do you carry a gun that I don't know about, and who on this green earth would try to kill us, and why do I have to keep my mouth shut?"

As far as Gigi knew, Mateo Salvador died in South America, gunned down by guerillas. Which wasn't far from the truth. He had been gunned down. But she wasn't exactly sure by whom, other than a rival drug cartel aiming to take down Hector.

Blair glanced around. Out here where anyone could listen wasn't the best place. "We will talk. At home. And I carry a gun for protection like a lot of people."

"You're hiding something."

For Gigi's own good. To protect her.

"We should call the police, Blair." Gigi gnawed her bottom lip. "I'm freaking out."

Maybe she should call them. Chief Deputy Beckett Marsh might be able to help. But then she'd have to reveal her past. Somehow it would leak and the town wouldn't see her as Blair Sullivan, business owner and honorable neighbor. She'd become Blair Sullivan, former wife of a drug lord who could potentially put friends and family in jeopardy.

Blair rubbed her hands together. "You don't need to be afraid. Trust me."

"Who was in that SUV?"

"I honestly don't know." But she had a terrifying feeling they would be back.

Gigi grabbed Blair's shoulders. "You think this involves Jeremy? Are you scared of getting him in hot water with the cops?"

Blair's knees buckled. She hadn't once thought it might concern her brother. But that might be the reason he wasn't answering calls and texts, or hadn't been by to see them in a few days.

Gigi led her to one of the many benches that lined the sidewalks. Blair collapsed on one, averting her eyes from the colorful wooden box of impatiens that sat directly under the black lamppost.

"Maybe we should call Dad," Gigi said.

No. Drug cartels were ruthless. Until she knew what she was dealing with, the fewer people involved, the better. "And ruin his Caribbean cruise when we don't really know anything? Let's not worry Dad until we have to."

Gigi stood and crossed her arms across her chest. "Okay, but I expect the full truth before the night is over. It's not fair to keep me in the dark, Blair."

No, it wasn't. Not at this point.

A blue pickup pulled over to the curb and Ronnie Lawson clambered out.

Blair stood next to Gigi. "Oh, great," she muttered, then bristled as he strode toward her with determination in his eyes.

"Well, well, if it isn't the little fox that stole from my vineyard." He shoved a wad of chewing tobacco in his cheek and pocketed the canister.

"I didn't steal anything. You should have been at the

auction today." Blair backed away as he shuffled forward, turned his head and spat a spray of tobacco juice.

"Truck broke down on the interstate. I heard it was gonna be a sweet one today." He glanced at her head and massaged his neck muscles. "What happened to you? Get into a major bidding war?"

"I wrecked on Farley Pass coming home." She gave Gigi a sidelong glance and prayed she'd keep her trap shut.

"At least you're not dead."

Yet. Her nerves hammered.

Ronnie made another step into Blair's personal space. "You know what I'm gonna ask."

Holt had given Blair and Gigi space, but he itched to know what they were discussing. Might be about whether or not to go to the police. Now, out of the corner of his eye, he studied a man with beady eyes and a receding hairline moving in on Blair. He towered over her and she inched back, then scowled. Didn't appear to be a pleasant conversation. Holt strode toward them. If this guy was messing with her, it'd be for the last time.

"Blair, everything all right?" Holt asked as he ambled up beside her, glaring at the big guy wearing a worn camouflage shirt and jeans.

Blair tucked a strand of hair behind her ear. "Yeah. This is Ronnie Lawson—"

"Own the sporting goods store outside town. You are?" Ronnie sniffed and spat a gob of tobacco onto the road.

"Holt Renard. Just moved here from Memphis."

Ronnie nodded once. "What brings you to Hope?"

"Opening a used outdoorsman store." And he continued to build on the tower of lies. "Chasin' the dream, man. Chasin' the dream." Once it hadn't been too far of a stretch, before his world flipped upside down. Once he'd wanted to major in forestry and settle down in a town much like this one. With Trina.

"I hear ya." Ronnie returned his attention to Blair. "So, can I come by and check out the inventory?"

Blair placed her hands on her hips. "Sorry you broke down on the interstate this morning, but I haven't had a chance to comb through everything myself, and you know—"

"You have a dumb ritual of having to see it all before anyone else. Give me a break."

Holt didn't like this guy. Manhandling her with his words and his stance. He stepped forward, ready to put the deadhead in his place, if for no other reason than talking ugly to a woman.

"Dumb or not, it's my thing."

Blair gave him an icy stare, and Ronnie chuckled. "All right. No need for daggers. Call me if there's anything I might want."

"You know I will. As always." Blair waved as he climbed into the pickup. "Ronnie Lawson is the thorn in my side. Greedy old jerk. I like his wife, though."

Gigi snickered. "He's just mad because he lost out on possible sporting goods."

Holt wasn't sure what was going on. The guy seemed too interested in Blair's purchase, but he might always be like this. Holt needed answers. "So, anyone up for food?"

"It's hot out, but I could eat some soup maybe," Gigi offered. "Blair?"

She stared at the road and chewed a thumbnail. "I really need to go through the wares from today and inventory it."

"You whacked your head, Blair. Take a day to rest," Holt said, wiping the sweat from his brow. It was too hot to stand around out here talkin' about stock from the auction—or anything else.

"Or let me eat some soup and then get to it." Gigi gave her the stank-eye and Blair heaved a breath.

"I'll tell you what," Holt said, "let's get a bite to eat and I'll help you unload the wares and inventory. I know you can't haul all of that out of the truck alone." He hoped she'd agree. He needed more time around her and access to snoop.

"I can handle it and it's a ritual I like to do—study each piece, and…anyway…" Blair glanced across the street. "But okay to something to eat."

So she wasn't going to let him go near that truckload of stuff. Why? What ritual? His suspicion rose to new heights. He couldn't drive her truck, and she'd refused to leave it behind. Was there something inside she didn't want anyone to see? Was that why the SUV had plowed into her?

They headed down the sidewalk toward the Black-Eyed Pea. Holt pointed at the diner on the corner of the square. "Cool name."

"Hunter and Jace Black own the place. Gigi dates Hunter…sometimes." Blair grinned, groaning when Gigi elbowed her.

"What about you, Blair? Who do you date?" Could a new boyfriend be into some bad stuff?

Gigi snorted. "Blair? Date?"

Holt spied Blair's cheeks turning pink, but she didn't offer a defense or retort. Would she still be grieving Mateo Salvador? He'd been nothing short of a monster with loads of money. It'd been over two years since he died. It had to be Blair's own decision not to date. Holt couldn't imagine the dudes in this town not beating her door down to ask her out. If this wasn't an assignment and he was positive she wasn't involved directly with drugs, Holt would be beating down her door. But this *was* an assignment. And personally, he was done opening himself up to love.

"I don't have time for relationships," Blair offered, glaring at Gigi, but behind the irritation with her sister lay worry and unease.

She had every right to be afraid and fret. Holt wanted to reassure her that things would be fine. But could he? He'd failed Trina. Holt had given her false hope every day. He'd believed with all his heart that God would heal her. He would let them be together and make a happy life. And in the end? Hope disappointed. Hope failed.

The day he laid Trina to rest, he'd also buried his faith.

They crossed the street and headed down to the storefront where red-and-blue-plaid curtains lined the lower half of picture windows. A large wooden sign hung overhead with black branded lettering: The Black-Eyed Pea. Home cooking, deep-fried deliciousness and the briny scent of seafood clung to the sticky air.

Hopefully, during their meal, Holt would be able to extract more information from Blair and Gigi.

Time was running out.

An hour later, Holt hadn't learned much more than the fact that Jace Black made a mean po'boy, could fix Blair's truck if she needed him to and might be into her—which flared a green streak in Holt that irritated and surprised him.

Blair had kept relatively low-key except to admit she stank at cooking. Now on his way to drop the sisters off at home, Holt turned down their country road. Only a few houses sprinkled in the area. A dark pickup truck whizzed by, kicking up dust.

A love song played on the radio. He itched to switch stations. The last thing he needed was a ballad about lasting love. He pulled into Blair's gravel driveway and cut the engine.

Gigi's phone rang. "Thanks, Holt." She answered the call and climbed out of the truck, then sat on the porch steps.

Blair exited the vehicle and Holt dogged her, stopping her before she reached Gigi. "If you need anything at all, I'm only across the street. Or better yet, take my number and call or text."

Blair huffed but traded numbers. "We'll be fine."

Holt wasn't so sure. "It's not every day someone gets run off the road and shot at. I'm not an idiot, and I haven't pushed, but it's obvious you're in trouble. And I want to help."

Blair fidgeted with her cell phone. "I don't even know you."

"Fair enough, but I'm not the one running you down with a gun. The fact that you're not going to the police tells me you're into some bad stuff—"

"I'm not a criminal!" Blair's words carried conviction and pain.

He couldn't help softening. "I didn't say you were, Blair." And maybe she wasn't. He was struggling to imagine she was. "But good people have bad things happen to them." He'd been a witness to that.

She touched his arm as if she'd known and felt his own pain. "Thank you," she murmured. "For taking care of us and giving us a ride, but please don't let what happened get around town."

Holt would never say a word. Not only because he was undercover, but clearly Blair Sullivan didn't like the fact that she'd been associated with Mateo Salvador and his criminal activity. And Holt wanted her trust. "I promise you, I won't say a word to anyone. I *don't* promise to stay out of it. You could have died. Whether I know you or not…" He scuffed his toe along the gravel drive. "I don't want to see anyone die." Couldn't bear it.

"I don't, either."

"Blair," Gigi called. "Did you leave the door open after

we got home from the auction?" Gigi stood with her keys in hand, staring at the front door.

Blair frowned and marched toward the house. Holt followed. "No. We didn't go inside and I know I wouldn't have left it open."

Holt nudged both women behind him and studied the cracked-open door. "Did ya'll notice that truck that flew by a minute ago? Either of you recognize it?"

Blair's hand trembled. "Not really." She looped her arm in Gigi's as if trying to hold them both up. Gigi shook her head.

He handed Blair his truck keys. "Go get in my truck and lock the doors. Anything happens, you drive away. Don't even hesitate."

Blair stared at the keys, lips quivering.

"Go," he said with a little more force, and gave her a gentle shove toward the steps.

When she and Gigi were inside the cab of his truck, Holt drew his gun, toed open the front door, then slipped inside. Not a sound except for the refrigerator humming and the air-conditioning unit working to keep the house cool.

Nothing seemed out of place.

He cleared each room downstairs and up. Everything appeared to be in order, but his gut screamed someone had been in here. And the culprit might have been in that pickup. If they'd been five minutes earlier...

Holt came outside. Blair and Gigi whispered inside the truck. Possibly keeping secrets and discussing information he desperately needed to find their brother and Agent Livingston. Blair opened the truck door.

"I didn't see anything out of place, but come in and take a look. See if you notice anything unusual."

Blair entered her living room first. "It smells like oil and exhaust."

Holt sniffed. "You're right." Definitely wasn't Blair's signature scent. She smelled like a bouquet of springtime, which irked him that he'd picked up on it…enjoyed the fragrance. He had one purpose in being here, and it wasn't to admire Blair Sullivan's flowery scent.

He walked the house with her and Gigi.

"I don't see anything missing." Blair shivered and rubbed her forearms. "I guess we did leave the door cracked."

Holt didn't believe that, and the way Blair was nervously rubbing her arms said she didn't, either. Gigi's narrowed eyes confirmed what Holt was thinking.

Blair was lying. But why?

Blair walked to the front door and opened it. "We appreciate you checking out the house. We're safe now. I'll call if we need you."

Another invitation to leave. The last thing he wanted to do. Someone had broken in and they could come back. Blair and Gigi could get hurt. Worse. But she was kicking him to the curb.

Shoving down the fight he wanted to give, he nodded and stepped onto the porch. At least he was across the street. "Please call me, Blair. For anything."

"I will." Her eyes were wide with fright but she closed the door, leaving a barrier between them. No matter, he'd just go home and set up his surveillance equipment and play professional Peeping Tom. He wasn't about to let anything happen to her.

TWO

Blair leaned against the kitchen door, knees quaking, throat tight. Someone had been in her home. Her sanctuary. Nothing was out of place. Whoever had been in here had been doing something else. But what?

Blair rubbed her temples and tried to thwart the headache coming on. Neck muscles coiled, she closed the venetian blinds on her windows, double-checked the locks on the doors and stood in the middle of her living room, staring into nothing. Moments later, she peeked through her blinds.

All was quiet.

A movement through Holt's sheer curtains caught her attention. Was he watching the house—doing as he promised and standing guard? The idea brought a breath of relief, but not enough for her to let down her defenses.

She tiptoed across her hardwood floor, willing the hairs on her neck to stand down.

Stopping in front of Gigi's room, Blair heard the shower run, full throttle. Good, Blair needed a few moments alone to process the events of the day and pray. Then she'd confess the whole horrible and humiliating story. She climbed the steep staircase to her bedroom.

She opted for a fresh T-shirt and jeans instead of a shower. If she could work up the nerve later, she needed to inventory today's purchase. She opened her top drawer and froze.

Inside, lying right on top of her T-shirts, was a white gift box; a red bow had been stuck dead center. She swallowed a lump and hesitated, then took it out. The intruder hadn't been here to steal something but to deliver a gift—a gift Blair was sure she didn't want.

Forcing herself to calm down and clear her mind, she slowly opened it. Shrieking, she dropped the lid on the floor and covered her mouth to keep from getting sick.

Inside the box lay a dead rat. Underneath, a slip of paper stole her attention. Eeew. She didn't want to touch the thing. She hurried to the bathroom, grabbed a pair of latex gloves she used for cleaning and psyched herself up to remove the note.

Don't be a rat. Go to the police or tell anyone about what happened and people you care about die.

With trembling hands, she placed the note back in the drawer, then closed the lid on the rat. She found a trash bag under her bathroom sink and used it to dispose of the box and its contents. She hurried downstairs and took it out to the big garbage can, then came back inside. Gigi stood in the living room, arms crossed, wet hair hanging over her shoulders.

"Time to talk."

Blair rubbed her brow. "First of all, let me say that everything I've done to keep the truth hidden was to protect you. It was all for your own good."

Gigi narrowed her eyes. "I don't like where this is going. I need to sit down."

Blair waited a beat and then balled her fists to her sides as she paced. "The truth is Mateo was a bad man. I didn't know it at the time, though. Not really. In hindsight, I guess there were some signs, but I ignored them. I was young and in love. But he had dark secrets."

Gigi's eyes widened.

Blair pushed back tears. "He smuggled drugs for his brother, Hector."

"Hector? Mr. Don Juan himself?"

"Good looks doesn't mean good person. I learned that the hard way. Hector is ruthless. Evil." Gigi could easily have been smitten by the man. A shiver ran down Blair's spine.

Gigi shook her head, then snapped it up. "Is that why you paid for that year I spent in Europe? To keep me away?"

Blair nodded.

"Until you said I could come live with you after Mateo died."

"I thought it would finally be safe." Blair had been wrong.

"When you found out the truth, why didn't you leave? Call Dad?"

Blair smoothed Gigi's wet hair. "Women don't leave Salvador men. And Dad might be a marine, but he was no match for a powerful drug cartel. I wanted to, though. Believe me."

Gigi hugged Blair. "I'm so sorry. You must have been terrified."

"I was," she whispered.

"Why didn't Hector...you know..."

"Kill me?" Blair massaged her aching neck. "Hector is complicated. He was angry when I told him I didn't want to live on his ranch and let him take care of me. But when I explained I wanted to move here to where Grandma and Grandpa had lived, he changed his tune. Gave me his blessing and offered me money to start up the business and buy a house."

"Did you accept it?"

Blair frowned. "Hardly. I wanted freedom. Hector's

gifts are like chains. I'd never ask him for anything. It's not worth the future debt."

Gigi laced her fingers with Blair's. "He didn't care you changed your name back to Sullivan?"

"Not after I told him I wanted to move to Hope and start fresh. Stay out of the limelight. Honestly, I believe God gave me favor in Hector's eyes." What other reason could there be for Hector extending such grace when he wasn't a gracious man?

Gigi rubbed her chin. "You think what happened today had anything to do with Hector? Have you crossed him somehow? Would he think you've crossed him?"

No. Hector wouldn't have tried to kill her. At least, she didn't think he would. Unless he thought she'd stolen something from him, but she hadn't. Confusion's web spun fast enough to make her dizzy. "I don't think so. But we can't go to the police. You see why now." And after the note and disgusting gift, she didn't dare.

"Did Mateo have anything to do with Jeremy's drug problem?"

"No. Unfortunately, Jeremy got into all that long before Mateo entered the picture. I hid it even from Jeremy. I had to."

"So what do we do?"

That was the question. "Right now you try to rest. Then we'll watch an old movie and eat some dinner." And she'd call Jeremy again. This could still be something he had ties to. "From now on, lock the doors. Don't be so friendly with strangers. And watch your back."

Gigi nodded. "Okay," she whispered. "But no more keeping things from me. Got it?"

Blair pursed her lips. "From this point on." Meaning what she'd found in the bedroom was off-limits. She had to protect Gigi. She was already terrified enough.

After trying to take their minds off things with TV and

a light dinner, Blair changed into a pair of work jeans and boots. Might as well start on unloading the items from the auction before the sun went down. She drove the truck out to the barn and raised the rolling door. A wave of musty heat popped her in the face, sending sweat trickling down her cheeks. She paused at a noise outside the barn and waited. Hairs rose on her arms and she could hardly breathe.

After what seemed like forever, she wrangled herself inside the truck.

She should have taken Holt up on his muscle.

"Hey," a deep voice sounded from behind.

Blair jumped and shrieked, clasping her hand to her chest. "Holt." So not telling him that she was just thinking about him. "You scared me."

"I'm sorry." He swept his dark bangs from his eyes. "Thought I'd check up on you."

In the barn? Prickles ran up her spine. She wanted to trust him. She honestly did. "Did you see anyone out there?" Or had the noise been Holt?

"No. Why? Did you?"

"No. But I thought I heard something. Must have been you or my neighbor's horses. I'm jumpy."

"Understandable." Holt scanned the barn and cocked his ear, listening. After a moment, he relaxed. "How's Gigi?"

Blair forced herself to loosen up. "She's doing all right. I thought I'd come out and work on unloading the truck, take inventory. Get a look at everything I purchased." As Ronnie Lawson had pointed out, this was her ritual. Just her and all the goods. She would determine what went into the store, and what would stay stocked in the barn, for now. She liked to imagine the previous owners and the stories behind the objects.

"Can I help?" He stood there, all broad shoulders, no

danger in his eyes—just tenderness and concern that nearly sent her reeling. Had anyone ever looked at her like that? Mateo at first. But it had all been lies. "I know you have a thing about going through it alone, but I'd really like to help you, Blair. In so many ways." His whisper clung to her insides, disarming her guard.

A few Appaloosas grazed near the fence. She'd meant to bring them apples. "I'm used to doing things alone." It was safer than offering her trust only to have it betrayed.

"I get that. And you seem completely capable. But… I'm here and I have two capable hands, too." He splayed them on his sides, his white T-shirt clinging to rock-solid biceps and chest.

Could she trust him? They were just collectibles, but she did love her routine. She also dreaded some of the heavy lifting.

"All right. Sure." She didn't like being out here alone anyway. If she was really alone. It felt as if a million eyes were staring at her.

She grabbed her work gloves and donned them, her hands instantly turning clammy from the insulation. "I might have an extra pair." She held up her gloved hands. "Over there on that worktable."

Holt nodded and rummaged through tools and odds and ends until he found some. "How long have you lived in Hope?"

"Couple of years. My grandparents grew up here. They were happy in Hope. Plus, I love the name of the town and I needed it—hope—when I first settled in."

"Where are you from originally?" He grabbed a tote from the truck, and Blair motioned for him to stack it near the back wall.

"All over." She laughed. "Military brat. What about you?"

"I grew up in Memphis. Spent a lot of summers in a

town like this. Glory, Mississippi. My grandpa was the sheriff and my grandmother ran a lot of women's groups... and kept me and my cousin Bryn in line."

Blair liked the way his eyes lit up as he talked of his grandparents. "My grandpa died when I was very young, but I treasure the memories. Grandma Viola passed shortly after I graduated high school. What about yours?"

"My grandpa died a few years back, but Grandma Mavis is still kickin' and thinking she's thirty and not eighty-two. I haven't seen her since last summer."

"You should go. See her. You never know how much time you have with someone you love."

"You're right."

Blair heard the heartache in his voice. Who had he lost? That was private and she didn't want to pry by asking, but she was curious. She focused back on the task at hand. "We can arrange everything in categories. After that, I'll log each item with a short description, how much I think it's worth—unless I need an expert. Once I nail down prices, I'll determine what will go into my store and what will stay in inventory."

"I know we're not supposed to covet, but right now I'm coveting your organizational skills. You should help me organize my store." He continued unloading totes, bags, furniture and garbage sacks full of junk.

Holt lifted a hefty tub and carried it to the housewares piles. "Clearly, you're in great shape, but some of this is seriously heavy. You never have any help?"

Heat crept into her face, and she brushed the hair sticking to her sweaty cheek with her forearm. "My brother helps out sometimes, after I've looked through it. But he's...unavailable. And Gigi mostly whines, so I don't even ask. Occasionally, Jace Black from the Black-Eyed Pea helps. Or Mitch Rydell. Have you met him yet? He's my neighbor. Owns those horses." She pointed toward the pasture.

"I haven't met anyone officially." He sat on the tub, took off his gloves and raked his hands through his damp hair. "Maybe you can introduce me around."

"Maybe."

"So, why's your brother unavailable?" Holt surveyed the barn, taking his sweet time, as if hunting down something. Or maybe she was being paranoid again.

Dread filled her stomach. Sometimes Jeremy liked downtime and took off on his own, but he generally called to check in. "I'm not sure. He's a loner."

"He live nearby?"

"Memphis."

"Cool."

Holt continued to pepper her with questions. Some she answered; some she dodged. "Okay, enough with the twenty questions." She wiped her hands on her jeans and surveyed their piles.

"I'm just trying to get to know you, Blair." Holt threw a dazzling grin her way. In the past, it would have sunk her to her knees. Not anymore. Well, maybe she felt a flutter.

Two hours in, the sun had dipped, but the temperature was still in the lava levels. Blair's clothing stuck to her skin, stray hairs that had escaped her topknot clung to her cheeks and chin. She headed for an old but working fifties fridge, opened it and handed Holt a bottle of water. She downed hers in record time.

"Not a bad unit."

No, it wasn't. She'd overpaid. But sometimes her gut told her it would be worth it—to take the chance. Too bad her gut was always wrong in the romance department.

A turn-of-the-century dresser with intricate piping, a few embroidered decorative pillows and a collection of what appeared to be gorgeous hand-carved wooden ducks—nearly a foot long and several inches wide and deep—still hung in the back of the truck, along with two boxes she hadn't combed through yet. "I'm wiped out, and I need to check on Gigi. How about we call it a day? I can log these items in the morning."

"Sounds good. Thanks for letting me help." He scanned the barn again. She'd noticed him poking around a few times. Was he looking for something in particular or was he simply curious?

They walked toward the house. Holt stopped in his tracks and slowly pivoted toward the barn, head tipped.

"What are you—"

"Shhh." He placed his index finger on his lips.

Blair's throat tightened.

The horses in the pasture whinnied.

Bullfrogs croaked from the nearby pond.

A feeling of eeriness seemed to creepy-crawl through the humidity.

Holt's eyes hardened as he surveyed the yard. Woods flanked her pond, and farther back was Mitch's pasture-land. Anyone could be out there. Fear slicked her bones.

"Stay here," he whispered before jogging toward the barn.

Blair wrapped her arms around her middle and concentrated on seeing beyond the black of night. Even Holt's silhouette had disappeared, but his voice boomed, "Hey!"

She heard the sound of feet running through the pasture. Blair's nerves jittered. Adrenaline raced through her veins. "Holt!"

He'd told her to stay put, but what if he was in trouble? She hurried across the yard as a dark figure jumped the barbed-wire fence and plowed into her.

Her vision obscured by utter darkness and the stranger's hoodie, she couldn't make out a face, but his gravelly hiss connected with her ear as he clenched her arm in an iron grasp. "Rats die. Remember that. And don't expect your boy-friend to save you." He shoved her and she hit the ground, knocking her head. Again.

Holt rushed to Blair. Kneeling down, he touched her cheek with his left hand as he still gripped a gun in his right. "Blair, are you hurt?"

She groaned. "No more than I was before."

Glancing up toward the house, he grinded his teeth, reining in his temper. This guy had gotten away. Again. "Give me your hand." He helped her to her feet, and ran his hand over her head. "No bumps?"

"No."

Holt put his arm around her waist and helped her to the back door.

Blair shivered against him. "Did you see his face? What do you think he was doing, prowling in Mitch's pasture?"

"I think he was hiding out. Waiting on us to leave the barn. Blair, I have to ask. Is there anything in your truck or the barn someone might want?" This was now the second attack since the auction.

"No."

"I saw him grab you. Did he say anything?"

She opened her mouth, then froze. Something brewed in her eyes and Holt knew it right then. The trust he thought he'd been building in the barn had shattered. She backed up a step.

Something the attacker said had her spooked. And it must have to do with Holt. "What is it? I see he scared you. What did he say?"

Blair looked away. "Nothing. He didn't say anything."

Holt let out an exasperated sigh and shoved his gun in his waistband. "Let's get you inside, then I'm going to take a look around. Make sure whoever it was is long gone, okay?" No point pressing her in this state.

Blair nodded and opened the door, stepping inside.

"Lock the door behind me. I'll be back as soon as I check it out." He kept his irritation in check. The longer she held out, the worse off it would be for Jeremy and Agent Livingston. But he couldn't tell her that, because he couldn't blow his cover.

Several minutes later, Holt knocked on the kitchen door and Blair jumped like a scared rabbit before she opened it.

"I didn't see anything but headlights down the road. Could have been the guy. Maybe not. Too far to tell." He scratched the back of his head. "I should stay. In case he comes back."

Blair's eyes turned wary. What had that guy said? "You know I carry a gun, too. I'll lock up and be careful."

Grinding his jaw, he surveyed the backyard again. "What if I said please?"

"I'd say I appreciate your politeness but we'll be okay. You're just across the street. Besides, I don't want Gigi to worry. She's had enough to deal with already. I'll worry for her."

And Holt would worry for Blair. Maybe he could charm her into letting him stay. "If you haven't noticed, I'm quick on the draw." He smirked. "And I run fast, too."

Her face relaxed and he had her. He hated the way he had to do it, although charming Blair wasn't all manipulation. He rather enjoyed it. Liked seeing her smile and getting to know her.

Suddenly, a new resolve formed in her eyes. "You can watch me lock the door again."

What happened? He blew a resigned breath and pointed to the door. "Get locking."

He'd have to watch from across the street or take up

vigil in her front yard. Not to mention, he needed access to that barn. Something had to be of value inside, and later tonight, he was going to do some sneaking around of his own.

Holt's hunt inside Blair's barn had been a bust last night. She'd padlocked the truck and he hadn't found anything he considered valuable in the actual storage areas. Of course, she might have put money, drugs or other questionable items in a hiding place before Holt had arrived to help her unload.

Now it was Sunday afternoon and Holt had to pretend to build a fake store under his cover. Blair and Gigi had gone to church this morning, which made it even harder to believe that Blair was directly tied to anything illicit. With each moment, Holt became more convinced she'd been targeted. Possibly from what Jeremy had found out and wanted to divulge to Holt. Possibly over something Hector had done—or not done.

This morning, he'd eaten breakfast at the Magnolia Inn and done a little surveillance, since Agent Livingston had stayed a couple of nights. He'd had lunch at the Black-Eyed Pea, hoping to hear some gossip that might help him somehow. All dead ends. He'd called his handler. No news in Memphis, either. Jeremy's disappearance was still being looked into and Holt had called his cousin, FBI agent Bryn Hale, to have her pull FBI data. Bryn had put her husband, Eric, an MPD homicide detective, on it locally. Just some unofficial snooping by his friends.

So far, crickets. Where had Jeremy gone? He'd asked Holt to meet him about some information he'd gathered— against Holt's wishes—but he'd never shown up to the meeting. That was over a week ago.

The door opened to his store.

"We're not ready for business yet." He turned to see Gigi holding two cups of coffee.

"Just peeking in on my neighbor. How's it coming along?"

"Hopelessly." Story of his life. "I need a vision."

"You didn't already have that?"

No. He had a budget from the DEA to make it look real and that was about all. But he had to confess, he'd enjoyed hanging fishing equipment and scouring a few pawn shops for items while doing a little subtle investigating. "You have any outdoor equipment you'd want to sell?"

Gigi shrugged. "You'd have to ask Blair. Didn't you see anything in the barn last night?"

"Not really."

"She just opened up. Sunday afternoons are popular with the tourists." She studied the store. "I could help you, you know."

"With Blair?" Holt raised an eyebrow.

A slow grin spread and Gigi waggled a finger at him. "With inventory for your business."

He took the coffee she presented and thought about it. He might have found a way to get closer to Blair. "You say Blair's next door?"

"She is."

He stepped outside, Gigi right behind him, into the summer heat and stared at Blair's window display. A winter wonderland. "What's up with your sister and Christmas?" From the store's name, to the Christmas tree on the side of the truck and the Christmas window display... in June, there had to be something to it.

"Ask her." She opened the door; the bell tinkled. "An angel just got some wings, sis." She motioned for him to enter. "I'm running over to Felicity's for a green tea."

He darted his sight to the bell and shook his head. Blair

stood at the counter, handing a stack of mail to a woman with long black hair, olive skin and raven-colored eyes.

"Thanks so much for this. I didn't mean to be gone as long as I was. I owe you one, Blair."

"You get a lot of mail, Lola."

"Mostly boutique stuff."

Ah. She must run the uppity-looking Bless Her Heart Boutique near Aurora Daniels's law office. Aurora owned the coffee shop Sufficient Grounds, too.

"Where were you again?" Blair asked.

"Visiting family. Out of state." She tossed her hair behind her back and shoved the stack of mail in her purse.

Wonder where she'd been traveling? He cleared his throat overzealously. Blair's gaze skittered over him. "Hey, Holt."

The boutique owner approached him with a seductive smile. "Lola Medina. We haven't been formally introduced, but I saw you at the Black-Eyed Pea yesterday when I got into town."

"Holt Renard. How long have you been on vacation? I could use one already." And a solid lead.

Lola's smile was clearly forced. Why wouldn't she want to tell him where she'd been? Was she hiding something?

"If you're looking for good vacation spots, Tijuana has an amazing nightlife. You look like you might be interested in that. And Tecate has a fabulous brewery and an even more fabulous spa." Her earlier smile eased into a suggestive one. "If you ever need a personal tour guide..."

"I'll let you know. That's all in Mexico, right? Baja?"

"It is. You ever been to Mexico?"

Not on the record. "Cancun. Puerta Vallarta."

"I knew you liked nightlife." She leaned forward. "It's in the eyes. I'm good at reading people."

He leaned in as well, until he was in her personal space. "Me, too."

After a lingering grin, Lola tossed Blair a glance. "Thanks again, friend. I missed being home...and the scenery."

Holt caught Blair's frown.

The bell tinkled as Lola breezed out the door and a guy several years younger than Holt entered.

"Hey, Manny. What can I do for you?" Blair asked, and wiped her hands on her jeans.

"It's what I can do for you." He set a cake container on the counter. "Sophia made her famous double-chocolate cake. Three layers."

"Oh. My." Blair touched her throat. "Tell her she didn't have to do that."

"You'll be sharing that with your new neighbor, right?" Holt asked.

Manny turned and nodded. "Manny Menendez."

"He's Sophie's brother. She works for the Drummonds," Blair offered, then did what Holt wanted to do. Slid her finger into the icing and closed her eyes to savor it. "This is amazing."

"I know," Manny said.

Holt stopped gawking at Blair's display and faced Manny. "Holt Renard."

Manny gave a nod of acknowledgment. "Well, Mitch has me shoveling hay today, so I'll see you later."

Blair waved her goodbye and turned to Holt. "What brings you in? You know I was getting cake?"

"What's the deal with that little saying?" He quirked his thumb toward the bell above the door.

"Haven't you ever seen *It's a Wonderful Life*? It's a classic Christmas movie. Bell rings. An angel gets its wings."

This woman was adorably strange and confusing. "Maybe. I don't remember." Holt scoped out the place. Decorated Christmas trees in every corner, merchandise underneath as if they were Christmas gifts. Even an old mantel had been secured to the wall complete with stockings hanging.

Colored lights ran the length of the walls and hung from the ceiling. "So…what's up with this?" He twirled his finger around the store.

"I like Christmas."

Holt feigned shock. "Really? I had no idea."

Blair tossed him a flat look, but he spotted a fair amount of amusement in her eyes. Hopefully, he could regain the ground he'd lost last night when she suddenly turned wary again. He hated to admit he really liked her.

"Everything in here represents a life lived. Those bowls." She pointed. "Someone may have mixed dough to make a Christmas pie or to throw together a birthday cake." She motioned toward an old club chair and ottoman. "A dad might have read his child bedtime stories sitting there, maybe *The Night Before Christmas*. Somewhere along the line, those memories were tossed out. Not wanted. I find that sad."

But what did it have to do with Christmas 24/7? Holt perused old books, hutches, curio cabinets, coins, knives, dolls and various stuffed toys.

He understood the concept. He'd kept some of Trina's belongings for years, then couldn't bear the memories and had given them away. He jabbed a thumb toward a kiddie tea set. "A little girl had a tea party and invited some of those stuffed animals."

Blair beamed. The first real smile he'd seen. It lit him up brighter than the window display. "Yes, maybe. And over there a grandfather taught his grandson how to play chess." Excitement laced her voice. She enjoyed this— imagining, pretending…dreaming.

Holt eyed the old table with a wooden chessboard arranged on top. Something about seeing her thrilled and happy set off a spark in him, and he played along to keep that smile on her face, the childlike wonder in her eyes. "And he went on to win the national championship to make his grandpa proud, but Grandpa died before he saw it and so the boy couldn't stand to play chess again. And he gave his memories away," he murmured. Just like Holt.

Running her slender finger down the chessboard, Blair slowly nodded. "Perhaps. People discard memories in the form of objects for all sorts of reasons. I like to think I'm giving someone a chance to make new memories."

Holt understood more than he wished to.

"You play pretend well." Blair gave him a nod of approval.

If she only knew how well.

Blair cleared her throat and rubbed her nose, reminding him of Jeremy's habit. Guilt ate at Holt. For keeping the fact that he knew Jeremy from Blair and because Jeremy's disappearance might be Holt's fault.

If something happened to him, how would he look Blair in the eye and explain?

"So, what did you need?" Blair tucked a stray strand of hair behind her ear.

"My store needs equipment. I'm working on building my inventory, but it's sparse. I guess I could set up a few undecorated Christmas trees and call it a forest."

Blair laughed.

"Gigi said she'd help me. I'm gonna take her up on it." If his intuition was right and Blair was as protective as he thought, she wouldn't want Gigi alone with him. She might be laughing and sharing a bit about her business, but being polite was a far cry from trusting someone. She wouldn't even let him in the house for the night when an intruder had been prowling, which meant Holt didn't have her solid trust. Yet.

Besides, he didn't want Gigi helping him. He wanted Blair. Which unsettled him.

Blair scurried behind the counter. "Gigi can't," she said, worrying her lip. I've—I've got her doing a lot of inventory and prepping for the launch of our online store. But... but I can. I'll do it." Obviously, she didn't want to, but would say anything to get Gigi off the hook. He wasn't proud of manipulating her, but she might be able to help Holt find Jeremy. And it kept him close in case whoever tried to kill her made another attempt. Regardless of why someone had come after her, he wasn't going to sit idly by and let her be harmed.

"Great. Where do we start?"

"Naming the store for one."

"I'm all imagined out."

Waving him off, she rounded the counter. "My store is It's a Wonderful Life. Because, one, I love the movie. It's the last thing I watched with my mother before she died. We watched it Christmas night. The next morning she went out shopping and died in a car accident."

That explained Christmas all year round. Blair was keeping her mother alive through the store. An ache throbbed in his chest.

Blair looked lovingly at her merchandise. "I never want to forget the memories of Christmas with her. How I felt. And it's also perfect for my store. The little girl who snatches up a princess doll knows in her heart that life got a little better. A hunter finds the blade he's been searching everywhere for and his Saturday mornings have turned—"

"Wonderful. Not just wonderful but wonder-full."

Blair squinted at him, nodding. "See? Use your perception and imagination. You'll have a name before you know it."

Holt grunted. What was the point of using so much imagination for a store that wasn't going to ever open.

Blair straightened a stack of old books. "I need to make

a trip to Memphis in the morning. There's a little shop about thirty miles away. A huge junk store. We can use my truck if you want and see if we can't find some goods there."

"Sounds like a plan."

"Oh, do you think you could help me unload that dresser from yesterday's auction? I'm not in a big hurry, but we'll need it cleared out before we leave tomorrow." Blair waved to a woman and young daughter as they entered the store, the mother threatening the child with no ice cream if she touched a single thing. Why bring little kids to places they couldn't explore? Never made sense to Holt.

"You got it." Holt had seen into Blair's heart a little today, and he couldn't find a single way that, with her sweet spirit and sentimentality, she could be knee-deep in criminal activity.

So why spend all that money on that one storage shed last Saturday? Ronnie Lawson said his truck had broken down. Holt wondered if that had been sabotage or coincidental. No way. Blair Sullivan wasn't a saboteur. She wasn't directly involved in drug trafficking.

At least not willingly.

Holt's gut twisted. He had to know the truth. Just what had Blair gotten herself into?

THREE

Blair had tossed and turned all night. Every creak and pop had her bolting upright in bed and checking in on Gigi, who snored lightly, as if they both hadn't almost taken a dirt nap. The gun under her pillow had brought some comfort.

She'd learned to shoot with Mateo at the gun range.

Querida, it is important to be able to take care of yourself. It will make me feel better when I am away so long.

Yeah. Right. Little did Blair know she was learning to defend herself from drug lords. But when he called her *sweetheart* in Spanish... She was so over sweet talk and charm. Blair wanted real honesty. She'd take gruff and unpolished over silvery prose any day.

"I put the dresser in the back room. Did you want me to haul the other stuff out? Some pillows and bric-a-brac." Holt stood in the store area, hair still damp from his shower and the scent of his soap wafting through the air. She had to ride with that all day? She must be a glutton for punishment.

Blair had planned on going to Jeremy's apartment today to find answers. Now she had to do it with Holt along. Maybe he wouldn't ask too many questions. But until she was 100 percent sure he wasn't dangerous, she'd make sure Gigi didn't go near him. Which meant Blair had to help him supply his store with merchandise—while keeping an eye on him. Everything felt too coincidental. Or the paranoia was getting the best of her again.

"No. It's not taking up much room. I'll get it later. You ready?" Was she? Last night, in between contemplating fatal scenarios, she'd thought about the way he'd slipped into her pretend game so easily. Behind those billion-dollar looks and the killer smile, Holt had some tender spots. Or maybe he was using all that for some hidden agenda.

I'm being ridiculous. Would a coldhearted killer talk about a boy playing chess and losing a grandpa? Confusion gnawed at her gut. She couldn't trust her judgment. She'd been dangerously wrong before, but that didn't stop the way she was drawn to him as he used his vivid imagination. The way he'd arrested her heart with the lovely yet tragic story. Holt had shifted something inside of her. But she'd make sure to remedy the feelings. Remain cautious. Stay guarded.

"So, where's Gigi today?" Holt asked as he hopped in the passenger side of her truck.

"She's helping out at the senior home." Which was why Blair chose today to check on Jeremy. She couldn't shake her suspicion that he was in trouble, and her sister had enough to worry about without being dragged into Blair's search for answers. "She's overseeing the weekly activities there."

Holt nodded. "How long have you wanted to own your own business?"

Blair eased by Farley Pass, the ruts in the grass still there from the other day. Her chest constricted. She glanced in her rearview mirror.

"Since I was sixteen. Before that I wanted to be a race car driver." She laughed. "How about you?"

"I guess I wanted to be what all little boys want to be.

A race car driver. A firefighter. I wanted to be a hunter. A park ranger."

"A police officer."

"What?"

"Wasn't that on the list? Every little boy wants to be a cop, right?" Adjusting the AC, she glanced at him.

"Sure, although a park ranger always ranked the highest on my list. Love the outdoors." He cleared his throat. "So, I was thinking about the name of my store."

"Yeah?"

"How about Clear Blue Skies?" He leaned forward, caught her attention.

"Not bad. But no cigar."

Holt snorted. "I'm bad at this. Naming things. I had a turtle once and I named him Slowy. Original, yeah? And then I named my dog Doggy."

"As long as you don't name your store Story." Blair chuckled and they continued their small talk, stopped for a coffee and fell into easy banter all the way into Memphis. He perked up and took in the surroundings. "So, what errands do you need to do? You said you had a few."

Blair turned into Jeremy's apartment complex. "I need to check on my brother. I haven't heard from him in a while."

"Why's that?"

"Wish I knew."

Holt continued to scan the complex with narrowed eyes and a deep line creasing his forehead, giving him a dangerous appearance. "Want me to go in with you? This doesn't seem like the nicest neighborhood."

"Nah, sit tight. I won't be long." The less she entangled him in her life, the better. If the people who sent her a dead rat thought she was talking to him, they might hurt Gigi. Jeremy could be in danger, too. She had to handle this discreetly.

"All right, well, I'll be right here if you need me," Holt said, concern lacing his voice.

Nodding, she unbuckled and jumped down from the truck. Climbing the stairs to Jeremy's apartment, Blair fished the spare key from her pocket then slid it into the lock. It turned too easily. She twisted the knob and the door opened. Okay, she used to keep her house unlocked, but she didn't live in an apartment complex in a shady part of town.

She slipped inside. The place smelled like week-old gym socks and rotting trash—it was a disaster. Jeremy didn't have cleaning skills, but this went beyond living like a slob.

Hairs stood on her neck. A TV hummed from the back bedroom.

Jeremy must have been gone for more than a week. But he'd never have left a place like this if he'd planned to travel.

The door creaked behind her and she jumped. Holt loomed in the doorframe. "Sorry," he whispered. "I got worried." His gaze swept the area. "And for good reason. This place has been tossed." His concerned expression overrode her irritation at him for not staying in the truck like she asked. Striding over to her, he laid a hand on her shoulder before he crept down the hallway.

"What are you doing?" Blair followed, but he threw his hand out to stop her. She paused, frowning. Was the same person who ran her off the road, shot at her and left her a dead rodent as a warning responsible for trashing Jeremy's apartment?

Holt slipped into the back bedroom and Blair opened the guest room. No sooner had she stepped inside than a towering figure lunged from the side of the door, knocking her to the floor with a crashing thud.

"Blair!" Holt bellowed.

The hulking man pushed past her into the hallway. She jumped up, rubbing her hip that now thumped in pain. "Holt!" Exiting in time to see Holt's fist connect with the guy's face, Blair gasped and froze.

The attacker's feet flew into the air as he sailed on top of the glass coffee table, shattering it into hundreds of pieces. Holt pounced on him, seemingly oblivious of the broken glass, but the guy in the mask clipped Holt's jaw and elbowed his ribs, giving him time to spring up and blast to the front door.

Holt growled and darted after him.

"Wait! Holt!" Blair ran to the concrete stairwell and stared as Holt sprinted across the parking lot like a madman, hot on the assailant's trail. Then she lost sight of them. She should call the police. Jeremy could be hurt. But if he wasn't—if he'd been kidnapped—and she called the police, whoever took him might kill him. She'd been warned. People she cared about would die. Gigi could die. Jeremy could die!

No cops.

Dizzy with anxiety, she leaned against the wall and tried deep breathing. Heavy footsteps from the stairwell below shot her heart into her throat. She looked down. Holt. *Thank You, God, for keeping him safe.* His intense eyes held fury and something she couldn't quite place her finger on. His dark hair had matted to his brow.

And then he bounded up the stairs and was nearly on top of her, his hands grasping her shoulders, roaming her face, her head. "Are you okay? Did he hurt you?" Urgency coated his voice and warmed her belly. And the guard she'd been fighting to keep up slipped, if only a little.

Blair wasn't sure how to respond.

Strong hands framed her face, his breath against her cheeks. "I lost him on the main road. Tell me you're okay. Blair? Blair!" He gave her a shake.

She blinked and found her voice. "Probably gonna have a bruise or two, but I'll survive. Why would you tear after him like that? You could have been killed!" She scanned his arms, a few nicks from broken glass. "You're bleeding. You could have really been hurt, Holt." She had enough people to worry about, to be responsible for. Had something happened to him, Blair might never have forgiven herself. "What were you thinking?"

He sighed and wiped his brow. Hair hung in his eyes and she reached up and swept it to the side. He paused, caught her gaze and held it, a connection sizzling between them.

One beat.

Two.

She held her breath. This man should not be doing crazy wonderful things to her emotions like this. She should be able to control them better. But his genuine interest in her well-being and courage only melted her.

Finally, he broke the charged silence. "Before, I thought you needed protection. But now I'm thinking it's time you tell me what's going on."

How was she going to explain this? "The truth is, I'm not sure."

Holt tipped up her chin. "Not good enough. Someone wants to hurt you. Someone may have hurt your brother. He hasn't been home in days. Aren't you concerned?"

Blair broke free of his hold. "How do you know he hasn't been home in days?" She never mentioned that. Not once.

Holt's mouth opened, closed. He glanced inside the apartment. "It smells like weeks-old trash and there's a moldy pizza box near the coffee table. It's obvious. And you told me he's been unavailable for a few days. Something doesn't add up. Talk to me." Desperation laced his voice, as if finding Jeremy was as important to him as it was to her.

Fisting her hands to keep calm, she trudged inside the apartment. A few hours in a truck with this man and his actions yesterday didn't mean he could be trusted. She'd made such horrible choices in her past. Could she make good ones now? But Holt could have been killed. He couldn't have known an intruder had lurked inside. Behind the danger in his eyes, something drew her. She couldn't place her finger on it. But after all she had put Holt through, he deserved some answers.

"Jeremy had a drug problem. But he's clean now."

"You think this was drug related? Someone in here pilfering for a score?"

Blair slunk against the wall. "Perhaps. I honestly don't know. He could have relapsed and gone off on a drug binge. But that doesn't explain an intruder in the house unless someone knew they could find drugs here. And the truth is, I can't believe he'd have fallen back into old ways. He's done so well."

What if Jeremy had relapsed? Drugs were dangerous. While she'd never done them, she'd been around men whose entire business was about them. Her knees buckled with the weight of fear and anxiety.

Holt reached out and buoyed her. She wanted to confide in this man, to lean on him for support, but she'd been burned badly by Mateo.

"It's going to be okay, Blair. Somehow it will."

This man, holding her, stroking her hair, made her want to believe those words. Not only for Jeremy, but for herself and for Gigi.

She pulled back, peered into his eyes. In those blue depths she saw concern, fear and frustration.

She was going to have to take a chance.

God, I can't do this alone. Please help me not to make the same stupid mistakes I've made in the past.

"Blair, I can help you. Let me help you. *Please.*"

She almost laughed. What was one lone outdoorsman going to do against an entire drug cartel? He'd have to be Superman. A hero. Invincible. "You don't understand." A wave of shame from her past flooded over her. The heat of embarrassment crept into her neck and cheeks.

"Help me, then." He framed her face, the coolness of his skin relieving the burning in hers. "You can confide in me. I promise."

Blair wanted to. She wanted to believe this man was everything he appeared to be: honest, heroic, trustworthy.

She hoped he was the real deal. The alternative was unthinkable.

Holt's heartbeat thrummed inside his ears. When he'd heard the kaboom in the guest room and saw Blair lying on the floor, it had sent a raging frenzy through his bones.

She had to trust him. To confide in him. For her sake. For Jeremy's. For Bryan's. With every second that ticked by, people he cared about moved further from Holt's reach. Terror rippled up his spine and guilt churned in his gut.

Blair was the key to finding Jeremy, and maybe even Agent Livingston. Whether she knew it or not.

If she was innocent, why not call the police? Why not even bring it up now? She was withholding information. "Have you filed a missing person's report?"

"No." She ducked her head, avoiding eye contact. "I thought maybe he'd gone off on his own for a while, but…"

He hadn't. The apartment's smell alone made it clear he hadn't disappeared of his own accord. Who leaves town without taking the trash out? Someone had Jeremy. Or worse. With the guilt Holt was carrying, he couldn't imagine how Blair felt. "Do you want to?" Blair didn't know the DEA, FBI and Memphis PD Homicide Unit were—unofficially—looking into Jeremy's disappearance. At least Holt had that peace. What peace did Blair have? None. She must feel like a roller coaster inside.

But he could give her that peace. And still keep his cover. "I could take you to the police." Take her straight to either of his good friends, Eric Hale or Luke Ransom— both homicide detectives and stand-up guys. He'd worked with each of them and now Eric was his family since he'd married Holt's cousin, Bryn Eastman.

"No!" Her eyes glazed over with fright.

"Why?" She wasn't involved in Jeremy's disappearance. That much Holt firmly believed. And he couldn't imagine she was directly tied to any other criminal activities. But she lived in the same town that Alejandro Gonzalez had been seen in. That was odd to say the least.

And for whatever reason, she was being targeted, whether by Gonzalez and his goons or someone else.

He was certain of one thing: no one was going to touch a hair on her head. *Whoa!* Where were these fierce feelings coming from? He focused on her tortured face. Emotions he didn't want to identify emerged.

"I think he's…" A tear trickled down her cheek. Someone had scared the mess out of her. She'd opened up some, if she could just be brave and confide in him. Trust him completely.

"Blair, you're in trouble. I can tell."

She still wouldn't look him in the eye.

"Fine. Don't tell me." Frustration leaped into his words. Not just because he was losing precious time finding her brother and his colleague, but because he wanted her trust. He wanted her to lean on him.

Even though he shouldn't.

"I—"

"It's obvious you're freaked out, but you won't go to the police." He softened. It was time to give her the peace she so desperately needed. "I know someone who can help who isn't a cop. He's a private investigator. And he could look into what happened. Maybe find out where Jeremy is."

Technically, Eric wasn't a private investigator. But if Blair agreed, Holt would take her to Eric and let him put her at ease. Let her know he was looking into things. Yeah, he was fudging the truth, but if it helped her sleep, Holt wasn't above it.

Someone must have forced her hand to steer clear of the cops. Saying Eric wasn't a cop might garner a yes out of her.

For a brief moment her chin quivered and her eyes seemed hopeful—something he couldn't even muster—but she tamped it down. Inhaling deeply, she shook her head. "Jeremy has a friend. Someone he said he could depend on. Could rely on. He helped him get clean and keeps him accountable. I need to find that friend. He might know where Jeremy is. Maybe they're together. Could you...could you help me do that?"

Holt's insides wilted.

Yeah. He could help her find that friend. She was staring right at him with watery eyes, and he wanted desperately to tell her. But his job said to follow protocol. He'd never been more torn. But he'd never once broken cover. He couldn't start now.

All he could offer was some solace in the form of a fake private investigator and his word to help her. "No one would have to know, Blair, if that's what's got you worked up. Don't you want some peace?" He surely did. "I got a vague look at the guy. I could even give the PI a description." He'd already called his handler on the way back to the parking lot after the chase and given him the rundown, including a physical description of the assailant. Maybe something would pop.

Blair squeezed her eyes closed. "Yes," she murmured. When she opened them resolve hardened her jaw. "But let's find that friend first. Please, don't press me right now." She darted away, leaving a cold void swirling around him. "Maybe there's a scrap of paper or something with a name and number."

She was grasping at straws. No one wrote numbers down anymore; everything was stored on smartphones. But apparently, she needed to appear like she was doing something useful, when she knew she wasn't. And that had to eat at her. Not being able to reassure her that people were looking for Jeremy sent his gut climbing walls.

But this was his job. He'd known that going in.

He just didn't expect to care as much as he did on a personal level. And at this speed? It terrified him.

Running a hand through his hair, he huffed and started digging. He wasn't looking for a phone number, but someone trashed this place for a reason. Probably the same person who'd caught Jeremy snooping. The same person who might have been combing the apartment for anything incriminating. They'd caught him midway through. Interrupted his search.

Holt would pick up where the attacker had left off. The second bedroom. He wouldn't press Blair about the police right now. They were already on the case anyway. But he was going to find out why she wouldn't contact them. She loved her family too much to turn a blind eye to what was threatening them.

He was also going to discover who was targeting her—that would help direct his investigation. Was it the Juarez Mexican Cartel? Another known or unknown drug affiliate? Hector Salvador himself? Or had Jeremy stumbled upon something entirely different at the trucking company he worked for? Either way, Blair was being silenced against her will, and Holt was determined to do everything in his power to keep her safe.

FOUR

"Bubba's?" That's the name of this place? The place I'm going to find all my outdoor needs." Holt stared at the sign in front of Bubba's with a skeptical look on his face. Blair held in her laughter, surprised she could laugh at all after everything that had transpired an hour ago. Holt didn't press her for more information, but he'd mentioned several times that they should go home.

What would going home do? She couldn't do anything there, and she hadn't found any further clues or phone numbers at Jeremy's. Did she really think she would? No. But she needed to do something to help. And if she couldn't help Jeremy at the moment, she could help Holt. She owed him that much, after the way he'd protected her. He'd been fierce. Determined.

But it hadn't been enough for her to pour out her sordid past and admit she'd made grave mistakes.

She'd opened up, then clammed up.

"Well, it doesn't win any points for originality, but it does the trick. And you need to stock your store." Blair shrugged and entered the old building. Aged floors creaked, and the smell of mothballs, must and rotting wood relaxed her. She was at home with old. With the past. Not her own, but that of others. Her past was a nightmare and her life at present was a vortex of uncertainty.

Not going to the police might get Jeremy killed. Going to the police would absolutely get him killed. And Gigi. Maybe even Holt. Who knew? Had she made the right decision, turning down the private investigator? *God, help me! I need Your wisdom.*

"There's no rhyme or reason to this place, Blair. How will we find anything?" He swiped his forehead. "Not to mention it's hotter than a brick oven."

Blair paused and turned. "I had no idea you were a whiner. Huh. Learn something new every day." She slipped down a narrow aisle of stacked furniture, magazines, old televisions. Holt, too broad-shouldered to fit, turned and maneuvered through by sidestepping his way down the jumbled labyrinth.

"I'm not a whiner. I'm...overwhelmed," he muttered. "I don't see any prices."

"It's all negotiable."

"I'm in Thailand again," Holt huffed. "Not even a box fan to circulate the air? Really?"

"I think they're selling some cheese to go with that whine."

"It'll be moldy for sure." Holt smirked.

Moldy like the leftover slices of pizza at Jeremy's. Another wave of guilt immersed Blair. She needed to be doing something other than shopping and battling her growing attraction to Holt. Okay, the attraction had been instant. A woman would have to be dead not to want to gawk at that physique, but his personality was becoming as intensely captivating as his looks. She couldn't afford the distraction. Someone out there was after her. Might even be watching her now. Chills ran up her arms and she rubbed them away. Should she take Holt up on that private investigator...and why did Holt know a PI? *Look at what you've done to me, Mateo!*

She couldn't blame it all on him. Blair had made the

choice to go through with the marriage so fast, even when she'd felt unsure. She should have realized that whirlwinds, while consuming, destroy everything in their path. Would she ever be able to love and trust again? Not that she was planning to fall in love with Holt. But someday she'd like to have a husband and family.

Right now Blair would rather give up her dream to find a happily-ever-after in order to guard herself against making more bad choices in the romance department. No choice was better than making a wrong choice, right?

Holt's hand rested on her shoulder. "Hey, if you don't want to be here, we can go home. I'd understand. And my offer still stands. Whatever you need." Tenderness resided in his shockingly blue eyes. His smile softened, and she couldn't help glancing at the cleft in his chin, taking in his square jaw, prominent cheekbones. His focus was on her alone. His thoughts were on nothing but what she was feeling. This must be what safety felt like. It enveloped her heart, sped up her pulse then brought it back down to peaceful. Calm. She drifted away into the moment.

"You don't have a single flaw on that face," she whispered as her face filled with heat. She did not just say that. Out. Loud.

Holt's grin spread. "I like the way you change a subject, Blair Sullivan."

"What I meant was..." That was exactly what she meant. "Let's find the camping equipment, shall we?" She marched forward, paused. "I appreciate the offer. I'll consider it."

Holt going to an investigator without her might be a smart idea. Her pursuers were watching her. How else would they know if she went to the police or not? But surely they wouldn't be following Holt's every move. Would they?

She and Holt worked their way into the second half of

the building, just as cramped and crowded as the first. Old motors, boats, paddles, rafts…endless items to choose from.

"Dude," Holt said. His eyes widened like a kid's at Toys "R" Us. "We're gonna need a bigger truck."

Blair chuckled. "Have at it, Holt. It's your playground for the day." Let him shop while she mulled over the possibilities. She could ask around at Jeremy's work. See if anyone knew who that friend was or if Jeremy had a girlfriend. Anything. She tossed around the facts. She'd gone to the storage auction. Nothing out of the ordinary had happened there. Other than her finally winning a unit she really wanted. Then she'd almost been gunned down.

Had Hector done something? Stolen from rival drug lords? Could this have been some odd retaliation? Did she dare call Hector? No. No way. Bringing him in would be dangerous. Especially if he wasn't already involved.

Holt interrupted her anxious thoughts with a gorgeous smile. "You're the best person on the whole planet."

"Have you met everyone on the planet?"

Grabbing her hand, and catching her off guard, he twirled her around as if she were Cinderella. Before she could help it, she let out the biggest belly laugh.

"After this, I don't need to. You're it, Blair." He disappeared into the fray and Blair worked on dissolving the catch in her throat. No one had ever told her she was *it*. He'd meant it jokingly, but it had done something unsettling to heart.

No. Way. You aren't falling for a smooth talker with flirty eyes and a smile that turns you to goo. So knock it off, Blair Sullivan. Knock it off. Charm is deceptive.

Yesterday she thought he might be part of a drug cartel or a hit man. A few smiles later… How fickle could she be? But it wasn't the smiles. They helped for sure, but it was the way he protected her. The day she and Gigi had been shot at and run off the road, today at the apartment.

Offering to drive her around. He had nothing to gain by any of that.

And the way he played pretend. It had made a direct impact on her heart, pulling at every string.

Holt stepped around the corner, a fishing hat on his head, a bright orange hunting vest and a pair of rubber waders in one hand, a fishing pole in the other. "Pay dirt."

"You know that's stock, not an early Christmas gift, right?"

"A man can imagine."

Another flutter. "I think a healthy imagination is key to living a wonderful life." Or the key to wishing for something you didn't have. It was a two-way street.

Holt dropped his treasures at her feet. "I'm making a pile. I figure if Bubba comes over you can start the negotiation process."

Which reminded her… "You said you've been to Thailand. When? Why?"

"Oh… I went on a youth mission trip. I was sixteen." He absently fiddled with the life vests. "Trina's hair…" He laughed. "If you have curly hair, you're in big trouble."

Blair studied him as he absently studied the waders. "Who's Trina?"

Holt's head snapped up. "What?"

"You said Trina's hair." Was she his sister? His face flashed with shock as if he'd said something he shouldn't have. As if he'd let some kind of wall down. Blair would know a thing or two about that.

"A girlfriend. High school girlfriend." He jumped up. "I'm going back in."

Just a girlfriend? Blair didn't think so. Not with the way he ran from the conversation, back into the aisles of equipment where he could regain his composure, resurrect the walls he'd accidentally left unattended while enjoying himself. That was exactly what Blair would have done. It told her another thing, as well. Holt had carried the same faith as she did at one time in his life. It was a mild comfort.

After Mom died, Blair's faith had slipped some. She still went to church and read her Bible at night like Grandma Viola had requested, but the praying thing dwindled. It was hard to trust a God Who took the one person she'd depended on most. Felt the most connected to. And so suddenly. Blair had never had the chance to say goodbye. She'd been asleep when Mom had left the house. Not even a last chance to say she loved her.

She was…gone.

When Blair discovered the truth about Mateo, she'd found her knees and prayer again.

Bubba poked his head into the room and waved. "Blair, what can I help you with?" She explained what was happening today and haggled over prices while Holt continued to hide behind towers of coolers, outdoor cooking appliances, tackle boxes and hammocks.

After two hours, they'd loaded the truck until every nook and cranny was filled. And for a decent price. Holt hadn't said much other than thanks.

In the truck, Blair blasted the air and turned the vents toward Holt, whose hair was plastered to his forehead. The look worked for him. "We can come back another time. If you'd like."

"Yeah, that sounds good."

Blair hated the tension permeating the space between them. "I'm not expecting further dialogue on the mission trip. I'm already tense enough, so I'd like it if we could move on and chill. Yeah?"

Holt's shoulders relaxed and he grinned. "Cool. Chillin' like a villain."

"Not the best terminology, considering one is really after me." After the people she cared about.

"Right. Point taken." He twisted his lips to the side, then back and repeated.

"What are you thinking about over there?"

"Another rhyming phrase to take the place of chillin' like a villain. The best I've got is cozy like posy. I'm not sure posy is even a thing."

Blair cackled, lost control and snorted. Her face flushed and Holt laughed. Minus the snort. Even his laugh was flawless. But she wasn't falling for flawless. Besides, she didn't have time for romance. She had to concentrate on keeping herself and her loved ones safe.

Hearing her laugh, even the adorable snort, Holt could hardly contain his feelings. He wanted to grab her hand and kiss it. A big, wild, fun smack. Right on the back of her hand. To thank her for the day. For the fun. Even though part of it had been painful. Walking into Bubba's—oh, he was so not done messing with her over that—he'd remembered how much he'd loved summers in Glory with his grandparents, spending every day outside. A piece of his love for the land and old, dead dreams sparked to life, filling him with a flu-like ache.

In his excitement, memories of Trina had surfaced and he'd actually voiced her name. Out loud. How long had it been since he felt her name on his tongue? Over a decade. Holt was a walking graveyard. So many dead corpses buried deep. Dead dreams. Dead girlfriend. Dead hope. Dead faith.

The even more frightening part was that the thrill hadn't just come from the building and rows of equipment; it came from Blair Sullivan. The way she smiled, like gentle ripples in the water. It was the way she loved her family, her town. It was the way she treasured people and things. The way she could be tender one moment and tough the next. When it came time to purchase goods for his store, she'd negotiated like a lion, not budging an inch. But then, when it was all over, she'd given Bubba a big hug and laughed at his not-funny jokes.

The woman was a ray of noon sunshine piercing his nighttime soul. It'd been dark so long. He'd been covered like the life vests beneath the tarp that day in the storage auction. But salvation was hiding under that dark veil. He'd spotted it today, felt the tug to come up for air.

The question was: Was he ready to unveil his heart?

No. No, he was not. He couldn't. It was too much of a threat. He had to focus on this job. Think clearly. Blair fogged up his world, this mission. Made him believe this was more than make-believe. That he was actually building a store, a new career.

He wasn't.

This was nothing more than a means to an end. To find Jeremy. To find Bryan. Or to find out what became of them. To find Alejandro Gonzalez and bring down the Juarez Cartel. He'd spent the entire day with Blair and never once pried into her past, which might be the key to finding his friends, to doing his job. It was time to focus on the real reason he was in Hope.

Blair turned off on Farley Pass, heading into town. Her knuckles whitened on the wheel. "No lights behind us," Holt reassured her. "We're free from danger."

As long as he was with her, he'd keep her that way.

"I know. I was thinking about Jeremy." She slowed down as something darted around on the edge of the road. "Deer. Gotta be careful coming through here at night or you'll hit one."

"Noted. Hey, my offer for the PI still stands, Blair."

She gave a weak smile.

"You wanna get some dinner before we unload my stuff?" he asked. Time to dig. Which felt slimy in a sense.

Interrogating her. Manipulating. But it was his job, and he'd never been bothered by it before—which also scared him.

Wait. He *was* curious about her. He could do this without feeling like scum…well, at least less scummy.

"Sure."

He waited a beat. "So, where'd you go to college?"

"Memphis State. My dad lives in Memphis, too. He settled there after he retired from the Marines. But mostly he travels. He's a big fisherman. Deep sea, trout, you name it."

"I like fishing. And Memphis basketball. Grit and Grind. Go, Grizzlies. I will miss going to a lot of the games now that I've settled in Hope."

Blair grinned. "I'm a fan of basketball. And fishing. But I prefer a small town to a big city like Memphis."

"One more thing we have in common then," he said, finding that he meant every word. "Maybe we can go to a game this fall." Strangely, he meant that, too.

"We'll see."

No, they wouldn't. Sadly, he'd be long gone come fall.

"Any serious relationships?" *Come on, Blair. Open up.*

"Actually—" She gave him a quick glance, but it was enough time to see the vulnerability in her eyes. "I was married. For four years. My husband died overseas."

"I'm sorry." He studied her face, searching for how she felt about Mateo Salvador's death. Mostly Holt saw regret, but also some fear there, and a sliver of anger.

She slowed down as she neared the square, then parked at the diner. "It wasn't a fairy-tale marriage. But I did fall in love with him. I was young. He was charismatic and smooth. Gorgeous. He was also a manipulator and a liar. He pretended to be something he wasn't, and I was trapped into one big deception that I couldn't claw my way out of." She opened the truck door. "I forgave him.

After he died. Can't say I've forgiven myself for being naive enough to fall for him."

Holt had been in the DEA a long time. The fact that she was here and alive was a testament to her bravery. Her will to survive.

She stared him dead in the eye, forcing him to hold the connection. "I won't make that mistake again. I'm long past my naive days."

Subtext. Ringing loud and clear. Holt didn't have her complete trust. He understood. Her past experience forced her to be cautious, calculated and hesitant. Obviously, she saw every man as if he were Mateo Salvador.

Holt wasn't Mateo.

A nagging guilt burrowed its way into his mind. In a sense, he was. He was lying. Manipulating. Pretending he was something he wasn't.

If she discovered the truth, she'd hate him.

But he was the good guy. He'd never hurt Blair. Instead of putting her in harm's way, he'd protect her. Not that she'd ever know Holt's true identity—unless Jeremy wasn't found alive. Then he'd have to come forward and tell her the truth. Holt wouldn't take the coward's way out.

But if Jeremy was alive, Holt would slip out of town and never see Blair again.

Mission accomplished. On to the next assignment. The next thrill. The next wild ride.

His throat tightened.

"I'm glad to hear you've wised up. I wouldn't want you to fall for what sounds like trouble again." The highlights of the day sank like deadweight in his stomach.

"I won't. Make no mistake about that."

They entered the Black-Eyed Pea, ordered po'boys—again—and then, after dinner, Blair approached Jace Black at the counter. Nearly fifteen minutes later, they were still talking. Funny, she'd barely said two words to

Holt during their meal, so his attempt to dig deeper into her life had been for nothing. Something about the way she and Jace eased into conversation, the way he tugged her hair and winked without her pulling away sent a spike of irritation through him. He strode to the counter and brushed Blair's hair from her shoulder.

She flinched.

Why could Jace touch her hair and get a grin and Holt couldn't? He gritted his teeth and bit back the rejection. "You ready?"

She blinked a few times. "Um…yeah." To Jace she said, "Thanks for the food. I'll think about what you said."

"Don't let it keep you up all night."

Holt wanted to punch the lopsided grin off Jace's face. What had gotten into him? Jace Black was a pretty nice guy—not a punching bag for Holt's frustrations.

Blair waved him off. "No worries on that end. See ya."

Holt gave the requisite chin nod. Jace returned it with a friendly grin. Not a single arrogant undertone. Outside, Holt couldn't stand it anymore. "So, what about his face?"

"What about it?" Blair crinkled her nose. The most kissable nose. He raked his hand through his hair.

"You know, is it…flawless?"

Blair raised her eyebrows but said nothing. Which was worse than saying it was indeed flawless. She continued to walk toward the truck. Holt was an idiot for asking. He'd be a bigger idiot if he pressed her. But the nonanswer had him relating to a shaken up bottle of Mountain Dew. He was about to come uncapped and blow.

"Because his lip pulls to the right when he grins, you know."

Blair pursed her lips and continued the silent treatment, glancing at him then staring straight ahead.

Why couldn't he shut up? He should shut up.

"And for a restaurant owner, his longer hair isn't exactly sanitary."

He was shutting up. Right now. This was ridiculous.

Blair's nostrils flared. Was she…was she going to laugh? Heat filled Holt's cheeks. He was a blundering moron.

Finally, she cleared her throat. "I didn't see you complaining when you wolfed down a po'boy in record time."

"Yeah, well, when you're hungry…" They parked around the back of Holt's store and climbed out of the truck. Holt unlocked the door. "Let me get the lights on."

"I'm going to unlock the rolling door for you and grab the inventory log from my store."

Holt nodded and propped the door open. Blair strolled toward her place and froze.

"What's wrong?" he called.

"My door's unlocked. I don't remember—"

The door burst open, knocking Blair to the ground.

Two masked intruders appeared. Holt raced toward the men, cuffing one by the neck of his long-sleeved shirt. He jabbed Holt in the ribs, but Holt hung on, slinging him into the store's brick wall. He barreled toward the attacker and grabbed his mask, but the second attacker punched Holt in his kidney, sending a blinding pain through him.

Holt caught his breath, turned and ducked a punch, landing one to the second attacker's ribs. "Run, Blair." Holt took an uppercut, tasted blood in his mouth. But he didn't bother with wiping it from the corner of his lips. Instead, he rammed the guy, throwing him to the ground while Attacker One forcefully smacked him from behind.

White lights popped before his eyes.

"Let's go," one of them growled.

The other stalked toward Blair. "Not yet."

Holt rolled onto his back and used his feet to kick the guy who wanted to leave in the sternum, giving Holt time to spring to his feet and waylay Blair's assailant. She grabbed a metal garbage can lid and whacked him right upside the head.

Impressive. Resourceful. Holt wasn't prepared for the surge of pride that washed over him. But there was no time to sit and analyze the moment.

Attacker One growled and sprinted down the street, the guy Blair had clobbered not far behind. Holt gave chase but lost them behind the Bless Her Heart Boutique. He jogged back to the store and, reaching Blair, ran his hand through her long hair. "Nice moves. You hurt?"

"No. Little scared." She heaved a sigh. "I've been inside. They must have just broken in, because it's not trashed."

What were they searching for? "Let's unload tomorrow. I think we've had enough excitement for one day."

"I like the way you think." She placed a trembling hand to her throat, and Holt did the only thing that came to mind. He drew her against him, hoping she'd find comfort in him. Caressing her shoulder as they trudged back to the truck, he leaned his head on hers.

"You wanna talk about it?" Would she open up now?

"No," she whispered, "but I will let you drive my truck. I'm too shaky."

Well, it was a step in the right direction. He opened her door, then hauled himself to the driver's side and drove them to her house in silence.

At the edge of her street, Holt cringed inwardly and glanced at Blair. She opened her eyes and perked up. She'd seen it, too.

"What is going on?" She shot out of the truck before it had time to stop.

Blue lights flashed in the drive. Beams of light caught Holt's eye. "The barn."

Blair raced across the yard. "Where's Gigi? No cops!"

No cops?

Did she even realize she'd hollered that? Holt raced alongside her. Deputy Chief Marsh and a man with a cowboy hat and horse looked up.

"You've had a prowler in the barn," the man said.

"Where's Gigi?" Blair asked, panic lacing her tone as she faced the deputy chief.

"She's not here." Holt rubbed his jaw. "Should she be?"

FIVE

"Yes. I mean no. I mean… I don't know where she is." Blair's hands shook as she plucked her phone from her back pocket and hit Gigi's name.

"I'm sure she's fine. I already checked your home. Nothing's touched that I can tell." Beckett's deep voice held authority. She did a double take. He usually didn't say much other than polite greetings.

The phone rang once. Twice.

"Hey, you back?" Gigi answered.

The knot coiled in Blair's stomach released. "Where are you?"

"I'm with Hunter. We rode out to the quarry. To talk. I think we're on again. How was the day trip with Mr. Eyes?"

Holt talked with Beckett and Mitch Rydell—his horse nudging Holt's shoulder with its nose. No point in worrying Gigi. She was safe. With Hunter. "It was…good. I'll see you when you get home."

Gigi's voice lowered. "I'm watching my back. I'm being cautious. Okay? Don't worry about me. Did you go by Jeremy's like you said?"

The knot was back. "Yes. I'll talk to you about it later." She hung up. The police were here. On her property. Whoever left the note would know. Hairs on her neck rose as she scanned the perimeter. They were out there some-where in the darkness, watching. Waiting.

"Gigi okay?" Holt asked.

Blair nodded. Everything was spiraling out of control. She headed for her storage barn.

"Blair." Beckett trailed her. "What is going on?"

"That's what I'd like to know, Beckett." She stood out-side her barn. All her organizing. Her meticulous care. Ru-ined. Nothing was left in piles or on shelves. Tears burned the back of her eyes. Endless hours of work, poof! Gone.

A steady arm came around her shoulder.

Holt.

"We'll clean it up. One bite at a time."

She couldn't fight the comfort he was offering. Couldn't push it away. Didn't want to. Not now when fear all but coated her inside out. She leaned into him for support, and he cradled her against him.

"It's a shame about the mess, Blair," Mitch said, sur-veying the scene at the barn. "I had Chesley out for a ride tonight to enjoy the full moon, the breeze. When I got to the edge of the fence I saw a couple of shadows, heard the commotion. Chesley heard it first." Mitch rubbed his horse down. "I hollered and fired a round on my rifle. Scared whoever it was off. Called Beckett. Again, I'm real sorry, Blair." Mitch removed his Stetson. Golden brown hair had formed sweaty ringlets around his brow. Even without his grin, dimples creased against tanned skin. He was one of Hope's most eligible bachelors. But, oh, how Blair wished he hadn't called the authorities.

Someone might think she'd done it! That she'd ig-nored the note. Dread crept down her spine, leaving goose bumps in its wake. What would they do next? And who would they target?

"I appreciate you lookin' out for me, Mitch. That's sweet." She choked down the fear threatening to overtake her. "Probably—" her voice cracked and she cleared it "—probably some teenagers getting into some summer mischief."

Beckett folded his arms over his broad chest. "This doesn't feel like teenage pranks, Blair. I expect answers."

Holt put himself as a barrier between Blair and Beckett. "You just got one." He put his face in Beckett's. "So do your job and investigate the barn incident. Round up those rowdy teenagers."

He was coming to her rescue again. Holt had to know as well as Blair that rowdy kids had nothing to do with this. Even Beckett didn't believe it. But she was grateful for the support.

Beckett didn't back down.

The two men stood nose-to-nose.

Holt's eyes held fire. Beckett's were filled with ice.

No point in making things worse with the authorities.

Beckett's eyes narrowed while Holt's jaw worked overtime. "So the teenagers who wrecked this barn also ran Blair and Gigi off the road the other day? Seems like they've really targeted her good for some summer mischief…Mr. Renard. Now kindly get out of my face," he growled.

How would Beckett know they'd been run off the road? She'd only said they wrecked on Farley Pass. Had Gigi blabbed to someone and the news had made its way around?

Holt didn't stand down but cocked his head. "I don't believe I have the pleasure of knowing your name."

"Deputy Chief'll be fine. Now, about Blair being run off the road…"

"What makes you think that?" Holt asked.

"Back down."

"Holt…" Blair called. Beckett was right. No point in

him going to jail. Getting locked up. That would be the worst place for him if Blair needed him. And she was discovering each day how much she did, which terrified her on a whole other level.

He glanced at Blair as if thinking the same thing and backed up an inch.

Beckett zeroed in on Blair. "I'm not some greenhorn, Blair. I'm going to do my job, but if you don't come clean soon, you're the only one who's going to be sorry."

"Is that another threat?" Holt hissed, and went right back into Beckett's face.

"That's a fact," Beckett said, then spun out of Holt's glare. "Now, if you don't want people knowing you've been shot at, which obviously caused you to *run off the road*, fix the bullet holes on the back of your Christmas truck." Muttering, the lawman stomped across the yard, slammed the door to his sheriff's car and peeled out of the gravel driveway.

Blair unraveled inside but kept her feet rooted to the ground. Why hadn't she thought about the few tiny holes in her truck? Somehow Beckett had noticed and put the pieces together. Good for his line of work. Not so good for Blair. Mitch stared at her. "Someone shot at you? Why?"

"What? Oh. I don't know what he's talking about," Blair lied. How was she going to get the bullet holes fixed without the town questioning her?

Mitch swung onto his horse. "Seems to me, Blair, if someone took a shot or two at you coming home from the auction the other day and then rumbled around in your barn, you might have something they want. Ever thought of that?" He kissed the air twice and lightly kicked the sides of his horse. "And you." He pointed at Holt. "Might not want to make enemies so quickly. It's a small town. Sorry 'bout your barn, Blair." He galloped off the property.

Holt watched as Mitch rode into the adjoining pasture. "I don't like him. And I don't like the sheriff."

"Technically, he's not the sheriff. And they're both nice guys. Beckett's only frustrated I won't let him help. Like he said, his hands are tied if I don't divulge everything. And now…now…" She was done for. Mitch had put two and two together in seconds flat. Maybe he should have gone into law enforcement instead of cattle farming. Beckett knew good and well teenagers hadn't messed up her barn. How far would he go to get to the truth?

She studied the barn. What could she possibly have? Had someone hidden something inside her truck during the auction? If so, why? Maybe drugs and her connection to drug cartels had nothing to do with this.

Holt crossed over the grass and tipped Blair's chin toward him. "Now what? Because you and I both know teenagers didn't trash your barn. You're keeping a secret, and it's the reason you freaked out over the police being here. Well, guess what, Blair? The police are now all up in this whether you like it or not. Marsh isn't gonna let this go and you know it."

Blair might have indirectly sealed everyone's fate. She had to come clean. "I was told not to."

"By who?" His voice was eerily soft.

"I don't know." She told him about the note and the dead rat.

He inhaled sharply. "Do you still have that note?"

"Yes, but I threw the rat away," she whispered. "They're watching me. I know it. I feel it." At this point there was no hiding anything from these guys, so she might as well accept Holt's offer for a private investigator. "I've got nothing left to lose. Could you still call in that PI? You'd… you'd handle that for me? I can trust you to do that?"

Holt released a breath and pulled Blair to his chest.

"Yes. Absolutely. Text me a photo of Jeremy and any information you might know. I'll get it to him ASAP."

"Thank you. I wanted to accept your offer sooner. Don't think I don't care about my brother. I didn't know what to do, but now…" She leaned into him and smelled the pine scent mixed with a day of hard work. So masculine. Safe. But she wasn't safe. No one close to her was. "Be careful, though. I don't want anything to happen to you."

"I will, but Mitch had a point," Holt murmured into her hair. "A very good point."

She reluctantly pulled away. It wasn't helping her any to stay against him, to feel his warmth, his heartbeat. She had to stay focused. Something was in her barn. Could it have been from the storage unit? She'd gone through everything, though. Nothing there. No drugs or money. Not even a single weapon. "Let's start cleaning and see if we can't find whatever it was they were looking for. We must have overlooked something."

A new thought crossed her mind. "I hate to say it but with Jeremy's past and the fact that he's missing, I wonder if they think I have something he gave me?"

Holt wrinkled his nose. "You think it's drugs?"

"I don't know. I go to the same storage facility once a month. I've never had this happen before. Why now? Why *that* unit?" She dragged herself to the barn. "We're not getting anywhere standing here. What if they found what they were looking for?"

"What if they didn't?"

Holt hauled stuff back into tubs as Blair reshelved items. Dark circles had formed under her eyes and her rosy cheeks had dulled. But she wouldn't give up, and that he respected. But it sickened him to think someone was causing her this kind of grief. "Mitch said he ran those guys off. My guess is they were going to finish off the barn and probably head into your house."

Blair shuddered and kicked an empty rubber tub over. "I wanted to be free. To come and live my life in a quiet town. Settle down with an honest man. And never think of drugs and crime again."

In her exhaustion, she was opening up a more private side of her life. One Holt already knew, so he kept silent. He wanted to hear her version. Not as an undercover DEA agent. As a man. A friend. A friend who might be feeling more than friendship.

An honest man.

Holt couldn't claim that attribute. Not when he was standing here lying about who he was.

A rustle sounded in the distance. Holt hurdled a pile of knickknacks and prepared to grab his gun from his ankle holster.

Gigi came into the light. "What in the world happened here?" Eyes flashed with alarm as she focused on Blair.

"Don't worry," Blair said. "Mitch ran off a couple of guys. It's nothing."

"Have you lost your mind? This is not nothing." Gigi scanned the wrecked barn. "You said you wouldn't keep anything from me anymore. I'm holding you to it." She zeroed in on Holt. "How much do you know?"

"Enough to also know this isn't nothing." He lugged a box onto a top shelf, but he scanned the darkness, a nagging feeling eyes were on them.

"What are we going to do?" Gigi asked, and helped organize the disarray.

Sighing, Blair rubbed her lower back and opened her mouth, then clamped it shut. Something was going on inside that darlin' head of hers. If Gigi hadn't shown up, how much would she have confided in him? She was more than words on a dossier.

Finally, she turned to Gigi and gave a watered-down version of the day. She left out the intruder in Jeremy's apartment, and it didn't appear that Gigi knew about the note or the dead rat.

It wasn't like he could judge when it came to divulging information. He was keeping secrets of his own.

Gigi nodded. "Fine. We'll get this PI guy on the scene, but in the meantime be extra careful. No police. Got it. Tomorrow, I'm watching the store. You have your hands full here, and I do believe you promised this guy help with his business."

Holt shook his head. "Don't worry about my place. I can handle it." Besides, he needed some free time to drum up some leads on Jeremy and Bryan's disappearances.

Blair reached into her pocket, retrieved a ponytail holder and piled her hair on top of her head. "No, I owe you for all the help. This is going to take more than a day, though. I'm exhausted."

"Me, too," Gigi said. "'Night, ya'll."

When she was out of earshot, Holt plunked down on a bench. "I think you should let me crash on your couch."

Blair tossed a clean rag at him. Not too tired to think fast, he caught it before it nailed him in the head. He wiped off his filthy hands.

"Why? You're just across the street."

"A lot can happen in thirty seconds. It'll take me at least forty to get to you." Bullheaded woman wasn't going to allow it, but that didn't mean he wouldn't press her. His mama used to say she picked her battles when it came to him. Well, this was a battle he was going to charge head-on. "I can protect you if I'm close to you."

"Don't forget, I have a gun."

"Well, great. That makes two of us. We'll be doubly armed." He grinned. Hoping his—as she put it—flawless face would seal the deal.

"No. And why do you have a gun?" She narrowed her eyes.

"Like you said, I live in the South."

She smirked. "Point taken. But no. I don't want you twisted up in this any more than you already are. You could get hurt."

He closed the distance between them in three strides. Framing her face, he searched her eyes. Controlling these crazy feelings around her was fast becoming an exercise in futility. "So could you."

She touched the hand that still cupped her cheek, sending his pulse thrashing. "I'm tired. Grungy. I want to shower and crawl into my bed and try to sleep." She removed his hand and stepped around him, heading for the house. "I'll text you first thing in the morning. We can start on the store, since you have to open up soon. What's that date again?"

Holt caught up with her. He wasn't opening at all. Disappointment slithered into his chest. "I'm shooting for the first week in July, with vacation season in full swing. You can help me create a patriotic window display."

She paused. "You really do have an imagination."

"I'm flawless, remember? Speaking of…" She never had answered him about Jace Black.

"Good night, Holt Renard. See you in the morning. You'll call your private investigator friend when you get home, right?"

It hurt to lie. So he didn't. "The minute I have some news, you'll know." Hopefully, it would be positive news. For him and Bryan. But time wasn't the best thing when a person was missing. And it was an even worse thing when the Juarez Cartel was connected.

Holt had seen some vicious crimes committed in their name. If they did find Alejandro, maybe he would lead them to the head of the cartel, and they could take them all down. For good.

"Thank you. Again." She nodded and went inside.

Holt waited for the lock to click into place. This woman was so far under his skin he might have to rent a backhoe to scoop her out. But if she thought he was staying across the street, she had another think coming.

He'd give her time to get settled and showered and then he was going to plant himself on her front porch with his pillow, blanket and gun. Period. End of story.

Let the war rage.

Blair stumbled through the kitchen to set the coffeepot for the morning. Every crack and pop of the old house had her jumping and peeping over her shoulder. No matter how much she tried, she couldn't force the goose bumps that chilled her skin to cease standing at attention.

Achy muscles, a fried brain and a sputtering heart were not the way she enjoyed ending a Monday. At least knowing a private investigator would soon be on the case gave her a blip of comfort. And of course, if she was completely honest with herself, having Holt nearby, knowing he was willing to do whatever it took to protect her, gave her even more comfort. *God, I'm so worried and frightened. You've been with me before. Be with me now.*

She flipped on the light under the stove hood and left a lamp on in the living room. Stopping off at Gigi's room before tromping upstairs, she knocked lightly.

No sound.

Her stomach curdled. She inched the door open, her breath shaky. Gigi lay on top of the comforter, snoring lightly. That girl. Too bad Blair could never fall asleep so easily. And with everything going on, she might not sleep a wink. But her body protested, desiring rest. The steep stairs creaked as she climbed each one with a groan.

What could have been in that storage unit? Whatever it was, it was enough to scare and possibly kidnap a person for. The one time Ronnie Lawson wasn't there to outbid her, this happened. Not that she wanted ill will to befall Ronnie. He had a wife and kids. Life had been going smoothly until now.

She turned the light on in the bathroom. Hairs spiked on her neck. She stood quietly. Listening.

Cicadas. A hoot owl calling. Crickets chirping.

She shook off the willies and twisted on the hot water. After her nightly routine, minus moisturizing because she was too tired, she padded toward her bed. Tomorrow she'd help Holt with his business and make a call to Jeremy's work. She glanced down at the festive print on her pajama pants.

Mistletoe.

Kissing.

Holt.

The man would certainly know how to kiss. There was no way he wouldn't. But she didn't need to be thinking about the man who seemed to have flared a spark of jealousy over Jace Black. Her friend and nothing more. Letting Holt stew in his questions had given Blair some satisfaction and amusement. Rarely had she ever had a hold on a man. If she really even had a hold on him. Maybe she was imagining his arm slinging around her at her house as being possessive in a not-creepy kind of way.

She hadn't imagined the way her blood had warmed and hummed all over when he brushed her hair behind her shoulder. It'd jolted her enough to make her flinch. How could a simple display do such wild things inside her? She sure hadn't felt that when Jace tugged at her hair.

Two throw pillows had fallen to the floor. She tossed them on the rocking chair by the window, along with a few others, and then she switched off the bedroom light.

Soft moonbeams filtered through the windows, glimmering just enough to cause odd-shaped shadows to appear on the cream-colored walls.

She tossed back the quilt and white jersey sheets and jumped into the comfort and security of her bed.

Something moved at the foot of it.

Her breath caught in her throat.

She slung back the covers and shrieked.

SIX

Dropping the box of microwave popcorn and a two-liter bottle of soda at the bloodcurdling scream, Holt wrenched the knob to the front door.

Locked.

On a rush of pure adrenaline, he threw his shoulder into the door. On the second try it gave way and he bounded inside Blair's.

He sprang up the stairs three at a time, heart hammering in his ears. He busted the door open.

Blair lay paralyzed on crisp white sheets, sweat popping along her forehead and upper lip.

A snake hissed and slithered up the middle of the bed.

"Blair." Holt inched forward, his gut clenching.

Her body trembled like she'd been thrown into the middle of the Arctic Ocean.

The snake writhed toward her.

Red, black and yellow. Slender.

His throat swelled. "Blair, listen to me. Whatever you do, don't move. That's a Mexican coral snake. It's deadly."

Blair's breath came in hollow pants. "I think I can roll off the side. I… I'm…"

"What's going on? Holt—" Gigi froze in the doorway, bat in hand. "What is that?"

"It's exactly what you think it is. No sudden movement.

Be quiet, Gigi. Go get me a big garbage bag and a storage tub." Holt crept toward Blair. If he made a sudden movement the snake could strike at Blair, killing her within twenty minutes. He'd seen it happen before.

No doubt now. This was the Juarez Cartel's calling card. But how did it relate to the storage unit? He'd think about that later.

Now he had to focus on saving Blair without making a single mistake. "It's going to be okay, Blair. I'm going to help you. Don't move."

The stairs creaked. Gigi was back. "What are you going to do?" she whispered.

Keeping his voice low, Holt explained, "I'm going to wrangle it into the bag and toss it in the tub." Hopefully, without getting any of them killed in the process.

"Good. Good plan." Gigi's voice faltered.

But how to toss the bag without the snake sensing it coming and striking. Hissing and agitated, the reptile was mere inches from slithering onto Blair's stomach.

Time was running out.

Using minimal steps, Holt shuffled toward the end of the bed, keeping his eyes on the snake.

It raised its head and flickered its tongue against the air.

Blair moaned, and her lips and chin quivered. Strands of hair had matted to her temples. He was going to tear whoever did this limb from limb. "Blair, honey…" he murmured. "Hang tight. It's almost over. Close your eyes."

"N-n-no. I can't. I h-h-hate s-s-snakes." She shivered again. "I can roll really fast. Maybe."

She wasn't fast enough to dodge a coral snake. Its tail swished against Blair's thigh and she whimpered.

"Blair." Holt kept his tone smooth, easy…low-key. "You're being brave, but you can't beat it. All we've been through so far. You can trust me. Completely." He inched to the other side of the bed, behind the snake. "Close your eyes."

He couldn't afford for her to flinch for even a second when he tossed the bag. If she did, she'd be dead. And Holt wouldn't be able to handle it.

Her gaze flickered from the coral snake to Holt's face. Terror and uncertainty flashed in her eyes. She had to know he was here for her. He was going to protect her. To make sure she was safe. From snakes. Cartels. Didn't matter. The desire to guard her had consumed him at the sound of her scream. He wasn't sure he'd ever be able to shove it back down and bury it. Wasn't sure he even wanted to. More than ever, he needed her committed trust.

She held his gaze.

"I won't let anything hurt you. You have my word."

The snake reared higher. He had to catch it with its head in the air.

Blair sucked her bottom lip inside her mouth, flicked her sight to the snake, then back to Holt. Her eyes slowly closed.

If this wasn't life or death, he'd have hurdled her bed and kissed her. He glanced at Gigi and nodded.

Thumbnail in her mouth, she nodded back and closed her eyes, too. He'd kiss her, as well. But it'd be way more sisterly and on her cheek. They'd both given him their trust.

Inhaling, he concentrated on the head of the snake as it rose higher...higher...strike mode.

Now!

He plunged onto the bed, bringing the opening of the trash bag over its head. It hissed and writhed in the plastic bag. "Gigi, open the tub!"

She squealed and held the large container open while he tossed the bag inside, then placed the lid over it and locked the sides in place.

Gigi jumped back against the wall and Blair collapsed into a heap on the rug by her bed. Holt slid to his knees, noticing for the first time she was wearing Christmas pajamas. Oh, this woman and what she did to him.

He brushed her hair from her damp face. "You can open your eyes now," he whispered. "You're safe."

She opened misty eyes and sniffed, a strangled sob erupting from her lips. Holt moved into a cross-legged position, lifted her into his lap and cradled her in his arms. She buried her face into his chest and he simply rocked back and forth as muffled cries dampened his T-shirt.

"Who is doing this to me?" Blair pulled away from his shirt. Not a stitch of makeup, and there was no way this wasn't the most beautiful woman on the planet.

His rocketing pulse paralyzed him.

He couldn't give her the truth without breaking his cover.

"I'm going to find out. That I promise." Someone from the cartel must have gotten into the house while they were working in the barn. Which meant they knew the police had been here tonight and they were sending a message. A deadly one.

"Thank you, Holt." Blair touched his cheek. "I'd have been dead if you hadn't come by. I guess you can scramble over in less than forty seconds." A pitiful little smile crossed her face.

He chuckled. "I was actually on your front porch. And I owe you a door."

"Why were you on my front porch?" She hadn't seemed to notice that he still cradled her in his lap. Maybe she wouldn't anytime soon.

"I had the hankering for some popcorn and a chick flick."

"You're lying. You were going to talk your way onto

my couch." A real grin appeared. "And I'm going to let you."

"Good. Because I wasn't planning on talking so much as doing." Her lips became his focus. "How are you holdin' up, honey?" he whispered.

A tidal wave of awareness ripped through the room.

Would Blair accept it if he did kiss her? He probably shouldn't, but he leaned forward until he was a hairbreadth away, felt her minty breath on his mouth.

The stairs creaking jerked Blair's attention from him and then she scrambled off his lap and put a couple of feet of distance between them. Gigi had left them alone in their moment and inadvertently ruined it. But then, he didn't want an audience when he kissed Blair.

When? No whens. He shouldn't be kissing her period. She'd muddied his mind. His objective. Unearthing feelings in him he didn't want to explore. Didn't have time to explore.

He stood. "I'm going to poke some holes in this tub. By now the snake's out of the bag."

Blair cleared her throat and wrapped her arms around her middle. "Where will you take it? If we take the snake to Beckett, they might do something even worse. This could have been in Gigi's bed! I'd never forgive myself if something happened to her."

"Then we won't go to him." Holt had no intentions of bringing in the local law enforcement. He needed to call his handler, confirm that the Juarez Cartel was in Hope and connected to Blair. Holt wasn't sure if the connection was due to her ties to the Salvador Cartel, or if Jeremy's snooping had led back to them and they'd caught wind of it somehow.

Another thought punched his gut.

The head of the Juarez Cartel was here. While he'd never been seen, he was known for killing his victims with the coral snake. Holt wasn't sure if he'd come in to bring the deadly warning to Blair—or to kill her himself—or if he was hiding out in Hope.

Clever, taking cover in a small town. No one would be scouring one-pony places looking for the face behind the Juarez Cartel. They'd been scouring major cities. Atlanta. Memphis. LA. Dallas. Even Mexico. Who could he be? How long had he been here, if he was indeed using Hope as his hiding spot? Before Blair? After Blair—and if after, was she the reason he came? To keep his enemy's family member within his grasp. The shooting had to be about more than vendettas or her barn wouldn't have been tossed. They were definitely hunting for something. But why place valuables in a rival cartel's family member's truck?

Unless they wanted to frame her and they were retaliating because of a drug war. His mind swirled with scenarios and possibilities.

Holt followed Blair downstairs with the tub in hand. Beckett Marsh stood examining the broken-down front door. He cast wary dark eyes on Blair. "Let me guess. Teenage mischief."

Blair's face crumpled, and she pinched the bridge of her nose. "Why are you here, Beckett?"

"Because I thought you might like to know that I chased a couple of men off from breaking into your store. See, I tend to like communication." He raised an eyebrow, jaw set, as his eyes roamed the tub Holt carried. Maybe he'd think it held items from her barn.

"Holt was helping me with some heavy storage boxes."

"So heavy they knocked your door off the hinges?" Beckett eyed Holt and the tub.

"I did that," Holt admitted. "We thought we were locked out."

Beckett massaged his brow and scrunched his face like a migraine had come on full force.

Blair couldn't keep this guy out in the cold much longer. Beckett Marsh wasn't going to let her, and if Holt could clear him, he might let him in on what was going on. But warning bells rang in Holt's ears. Why was Beckett Marsh out this late running around town? He was either investigating or lying.

It was Saturday and almost a week had passed since the snake attack and the attempted break-in at Blair's store. Beckett had been breathing down her neck for answers. Answers she refused to give. Was he poking around on his own? If so, it wouldn't be hard to find out about Blair's past. That she'd been married to Mateo Salvador. If he knew, he was keeping it to himself. For now. The whole town might find out and the shame would be overwhelming. She'd have to move. Give up her business. She loved Hope and didn't want to leave. Ever.

Speaking of not leaving, Holt had spent every night on her couch, coming in late. On several days, he'd gone out of town hunting down wares for his store, and he let her know he'd seen Eric Hale, the private investigator. He was already moving on the case, but no news so far.

Dad had called from Antigua and mentioned that Jeremy hadn't been answering his calls, either. All Blair offered was that Jeremy hadn't relapsed. She hoped it was true, but she didn't want to worry Dad or bring him home to danger. Staying on his trip was the safest place for him.

The only time Blair felt any measure of safety was when Holt was in the house. Crazy how one man could do that—make her feel secure from evil drug lords. She touched her lips. He'd almost kissed her that night. She recognized the signs. Felt the chemistry between them.

Blair didn't believe Holt was a bad guy or connected to what was going on. He'd proven he could be trusted.

But kissing him wouldn't have been fair. Nothing about this was fair to Holt. She was willingly letting him risk his life for her, and every single day she felt guilty for it. Her life was in danger, and so was anyone close to her. That meant Holt. When this whole nightmare was over, then she could think about romance and falling in love. Now she had to think about keeping everyone she cared about safe—including him.

But it was hard not thinking about Holt in a romantic way. In a short time, she'd come to long for him at the end of the day, sit on the back porch and unwind with a glass of lemonade and talk. She'd come to depend on him. He'd fixed her front door and taken her box truck into Memphis to have the bullet holes fixed. They'd shared meals at the Black-Eyed Pea, since neither of them had much skill in the kitchen. Except omelets. Holt could make a fantastic omelet, but she liked when she woke first and tiptoed downstairs to peek in on him sleeping soundly on her sofa.

Hair the color of and as soft as raven feathers hanging in his eyes. The I-need-a-haircut look suited him perfectly. She'd been tempted on more than one occasion to press her finger into the cleft of his chin while he slept. Instead, she'd made coffee and opened up a bag of muffins because she couldn't bake, either.

She could make a mean pot of coffee, though. But right now she'd let someone else make her a cup. She parked across the street from Sufficient Grounds and walked over. Before she even entered, French roast wafted into her nose. The morning had started early for her and Holt today. They could both use some caffeine.

A local high school girl worked the counter, taking coffee and pastry orders. Owner Aurora Daniels sat at a table by the window with her laptop open, a coffee beside it, perusing what looked to be online documents. She glanced up and gave Blair a watered-down smile. That woman was a mystery.

"Sophia, your order's up."

Sophia Menendez popped out from a corner by a plant, bright eyes, long lashes. "Hey, Blair. How are you? I heard about your accident."

Which one?

"I wrecked Manny's work truck this past winter on Farley Pass. Iced over. Scared me half to death." She took her coffees. "Glad you're okay."

And Blair was glad the town still thought she simply lost control of the big truck. She nodded. "Me, too. Riella offered me your enchiladas. Twice, actually."

"My *abuela* made the best enchiladas, but I lost her when I was only twelve. So anytime. Gives me another reason to think about all the good memories."

"I miss my grandmother, too. At least she got to see me graduate high school before she passed. I'm glad you have fond memories, but I hope I don't have any more accidents that might warrant the hospitality."

"I hope not, too." Sophia waved. "Manny's back. Gotta go."

Blair waved at her Don Juan brother. She'd had Don Juan once. Never again. Stepping up to the counter, she gave her order and then headed for Holt's store. His back was to her as he talked on the phone.

"Right. I am…I'm well aware…The lake?…I'll check it out this after—" He turned and spotted Blair. "I gotta go."

Blair got that funny feeling she'd had around Mateo on occasions when he'd been hiding something.

No, just paranoia. Holt wasn't anything like Mateo. He wouldn't keep secrets.

She held up the coffee and managed a smile.

"I appreciate it. Thanks." He hung up.

"No problem at all."

Holt smiled, but he wouldn't make eye contact with her. "Like I said, you're the best person on the whole planet."

"What do you need to check out at the lake?" She set his cup on the counter as he kneaded his neck muscles. "And what are you well aware of?"

He finally looked at her. "That I need to be familiar with the lake. Tourists and all, so I'm going to check it out."

He never shifted his sight. He wouldn't lie. Blair's stomach churned with warning, though. "That's true. They might ask for the best fishing spots. I'll go with you. I'm familiar with the area."

"Great. I don't want to get lost." He smiled, but Blair thought she caught a hint of hesitation in his eyes.

Holt placed a tackle box on the shelf behind the counter.

"Any recent news from your PI guy?" Blair asked.

Holt's eyes held sympathy. "Jeremy hasn't been home or seen at work. He hasn't called or picked up a paycheck."

Blair's hope deflated. "Something's happened, hasn't it?"

Holt rubbed her shoulder. "Let's not think the worst."

"What about the friend? Has this Eric guy been able to find out who Jeremy's trusted friend was?" If they could find him, he might know something or at least give them a lead.

Holt's eyes flashed with an emotion she couldn't quite grasp. "The best guess was it was a guy who helped him with rehab. He was a mentor and maybe he even accompanied him to some Narcotics Anonymous meetings. Jeremy hasn't been to any recently. The last one was…was three weeks ago. According to reputable sources, Jeremy was clean. He was doing well and trying to make up for some past mistakes." His Adam's apple bobbed as if it pained him to reveal these things.

"If this friend was so upstanding and good, why keep him a secret?" Blair couldn't figure that out.

Holt toyed with the yellow stopper in his coffee cup lid. "I'm sure he had really solid reasons." He let out a breath. "He talked about you. I mean, from what the PI found out."

"He did?" Jeremy was a private guy. Never expressed himself well. Much like Dad. So unlike Mom. "Did…did he say what was said?"

Holt's jaw pulsed. "He said you never gave up on him. Even when you'd been going through your own troubles, you called him. Checked in on him. Made sure he had food in his fridge when you came up for visits."

Blair's throat constricted. "That's so nice."

"Apparently, he called you a Good Samaritan. Said while he should have been taking care of you, you were taking care of everyone else. He knows you love him." Holt's voice had turned husky. He tossed his stopper in the trash and raked a hand through his hair.

Speaking of a tortured soul, right now Holt appeared to be one, too. Maybe he was thinking about Trina. Losing her. Blair pushed back the threatening tears. Knowing Jeremy fully understood how much she loved him was a comfort.

Knowing he loved her and had spoken about her meant the world. Now if she could only tell him out loud how much she loved him. She was losing hope.

Holt slapped the counter with his palm. "You know what? Let's hit the lake now. Sooner is better, right?"

"You want to explore Hope Lake now?"

"Yes, I do. We can pack a picnic basket, and since we both know you can't cook, you can go by the Black-Eyed

Pea. Better yet, I'll go by there." The corner of his mouth tipped up.

Blair melted like custard on a hot day. If he was offering picnics, he couldn't have been hiding something. Her paranoia evaporated. "You want to turn this lake exploration into a picnic? That will eat up most of the day. You sure?"

"I'm sure. I want to have a picnic. And I want to go with you. I'll hook that johnboat on my trailer and we can be out there in an hour. What do you say?"

"Are you for real?"

"Blair, Eric is doing everything he can. If anyone can find Jeremy, it's him. When he has a lead, he'll call me. Are we going to let whoever's after you rule your life? Let's go live a little. Just for a while."

A lake day. The weather was in the mideighties and breezy. A rarity in June. "Okay, and I'll go get the picnic supplies and pretend you didn't tell me I couldn't cook."

Holt brushed her hair off her face and gave her an odd expression that sent ripples through her stomach. "Okay, but no gazing on flawless faces while you're in there. And order me two sandwiches. I'll be starving."

Blair nodded because she flat-out couldn't speak. She headed out the door, popped in to tell Gigi she had to man the store the rest of the day and then she waltzed down the street to grab their food.

A sudden cold chill swept from her lower back to her neck. Pausing, she glanced around. The town was full of tourists, locals out shopping and passing a Saturday away.

But she couldn't shake the feeling someone was watching her.

SEVEN

Holt was going to need a bell on his door, too. Blair had overheard him talking to his handler at the DEA. Apparently, Bryan Livingston had been lying low at a cabin near Hope Lake. Holt hadn't had a chance to skulk around out there yet.

Now he'd have to do it with Blair by his side. Suspicion had been written all over her face. What if she would have asked who he'd been talking to? The lying was becoming harder with each moment. He'd been trying to separate his personal feelings from professional, but he was failing.

Every day, he found himself caring more for Blair.

As they launched the boat out into water, Holt realized that Hope Lake was anything but small. He counted about a dozen boats, some full of fishermen and others carrying teenagers passing a lazy day away. A few families were grilling on pontoon boats. Holt inhaled the fishy air, the aroma of burgers and hotdogs and sunshine. The breeze off the lake was perfection. And there was just enough heat to make him want to take a nap as the boat lulled along the green waters.

But sleeping while Blair perched beside him? Never gonna happen. Maybe after a while on the lake he could interest her in a hike through the woods, and while she enjoyed nature, Holt would hunt for clues, and by clues, he meant Bryan's body. A sinking sensation flooded his gut.

Blair reclined at the front of the boat, letting her fingers skim the water. Her long, dark hair hung over her face, the sun bringing out its golden highlights. Sun-kissed skin, long legs and a heart that was twice as big as this lake. A heart that had finally given Holt its trust.

And with every lie he told, he was crushing it. Could she ever forgive him if she did find out the truth?

Every day this week, as he built his fake business, his imagination had run wild and he almost believed this was his life. It was supposed to have been. Before Trina died and his world and future crumbled. He'd shoved the pain, his faith and all thoughts of God down deep, but out here on the water with the pine trees and blue skies, he couldn't forget there was a God. He couldn't forget all the wonderful experiences he'd had in his early teens when his faith was strong.

Now that things were shifting in his heart, those feelings, along with the painful ones, were surfacing. Holt had made his choice. Chosen a career that kept him in the line of fire, kept him taking risks and pulled him away for long periods of time. No time to think about finding someone new. But here. Now. It was like those dreams were resurrecting. Like hope was wiggling its way out of the coffin Holt had nailed shut when he was eighteen.

"I can't see your eyes under those tinted glasses. What are you thinking?" Blair asked.

"I was thinking this is the most perfect day I've had in a long time. I'm glad we did this." Holt kicked his feet up and rested his hands on the back of his neck. "How about you?"

"I was wondering why you aren't already in a relationship."

Blair had been honest with him about Mateo. Since he'd

been bunking on her couch, she'd opened up even more about her past. Holt owed her, and…and he wanted her to know him. Who Holt *McKnight* was. He dropped his feet and leaned forward, his hands on his knees. "I thought I was going to marry Trina—my high school sweetheart. Settle down. Have a brood of kids. But she died of cancer our senior year."

"I'm so sorry, Holt."

He rubbed the back of his neck. "I haven't talked about her. Until you. Is that weird?"

Blair squeezed his hand. "I hope it means you feel comfortable. I'd like to hear about her. If you want to talk."

He'd been so bent on keeping Blair safe it didn't cross his mind that she could make him feel safe, too. But she did. How strange. And wonderful. "People thought she was outgoing and a social butterfly because she was a cheerleader, but she was actually shy. Her mom pressed her to cheer. She never liked it and always had a panic attack before games. That's how we got to be friends. I found her wigging out behind the concession stand before lineup."

Blair chuckled. "Sounds like the start to a romantic young adult novel."

"It was. I mean, I guess. I don't read many books."

"Love at first sight, huh?"

Holt relaxed, laughed even. He hadn't been able to share memories about Trina, let alone laugh about them in…ever. "No. I thought she was cute but it wasn't a knock-my-breath-away kind of love affair. I started helping her with the panic attacks and then tutored her in math."

"You were the smart guy."

"I was the fullback on the football team. *And* smart. Are you stereotyping me?"

Blair reached into the picnic basket and handed Holt a

ham and cheese on wheat. They spent the next hour floating along the lake, eating and sharing memories. Unpacking the past released a weight from Holt's chest. Blair listened intently, asked questions and never judged.

"Thank you for sharing Trina with me. I've learned a lot about you. Not every young boy would stick by a sick girl's side."

"I thought God would heal her. Told her that every day. Up until the very end. He didn't." Holt wadded his napkin in his hand. He'd been told that God had a bigger plan. Blah, blah, blah. Still hadn't made him feel any better.

"Would you be interested in going to church with me tomorrow?" she asked over a piece of peach cobbler.

He nearly choked on a peach slice. Church? He hadn't been in the house of God in years. The thought of church with Blair didn't turn his stomach, it just shocked him. Would God even care if he came to church? The talk of his past sent a wave of loneliness through him. He missed God. Missed the old friendship Holt had severed. "Okay. Yeah. Let's do it."

She nodded and placed their empty containers and trash in the picnic basket. He studied the way she moved. Everything about her was seasoned with grace and gentleness. She stirred his insides.

Closing the basket, she sat beside him, her sweet scent drawing him toward her, like a tiny bread crumb he needed to follow. "I guess you never get over the one true love of your life."

Holt hadn't thought he would ever get over Trina. He'd never allowed himself to. But lately...since coming to Hope...

Clasping Blair's delicate wrist, he drew her to him, then slid his sunglasses onto his head. "You don't forget them, but I think you do get to move on. And I'm not sure you only get *one* true love. That seems cruel."

Blair licked her bottom lip. "That does. I don't think God's cruel."

Holt wasn't so sure he still thought God was cruel, either. Not when He'd created something as unique and wonderful as Blair. He studied her face, trying to memorize every feature.

"No," he whispered. "Blair..." He threaded his hand into her silky hair and guided her lips to his.

A *crack* sounded above his head; bark splintered on a tree near the cove they'd been floating in.

"Get down!" Holt hollered, and dove for his tackle box, grabbing his gun.

Another shot fired and clipped the trolling motor. No way they could paddle faster than a bullet.

"Tell me you can swim, Blair." Holt shielded her with his body, too afraid to fire back. What if he hit a bystander hiking in the woods? Thankfully, the area they were in at the moment was secluded and set along a bank that led into dense woods all around.

"I can."

"Great. Go. Over the side and swim for the shore. I'm right behind you." Not exactly the way he wanted to go on an investigative hike. Holt helped her scramble over the side with a splash. "Keep swimming. Don't look back."

Bullets sprayed the water near the boat. Holt had no choice. He fired in the direction the shot came from and dove into the water, keeping his gun from getting wet. Maybe the returned fire would buy them time to get into the shelter of the woods.

Holt pumped his one arm, swimming backward. Good thing he had a cousin who'd kept him competitive in swimming. He was no Bryn, but he could hold his own in the water. He fired another shot, trying to conserve his bullets in case he needed more in the minutes to come.

Blair was almost to shore when she grunted and yelped. "I'm—I'm stuck! My foot's twisted in roots or something."

Holt tossed his gun to shore and went under to untangle Blair's foot. Something had her bound. He couldn't see well in the murky water. He came up, grabbed a breath and went back under.

Blair screamed again. Another round of shots must have been fired. She came under the water with him and they worked together to unlatch whatever had her tangled.

Holt pulled with everything he had in him. Rope gave way and Blair's foot released. He motioned for her to go, to swim on to freedom. She nodded and then her eyes widened and her mouth opened. Bubbles sprayed out with her gurgled wail.

Please don't let it be another snake.

Lungs burning, Holt turned and jerked backward.

Agent Bryan Livingston.

Holt held in his own scream at seeing the bloated body weighted down by concrete and rope, the same rope that had snared Blair. His stomach turned. He pointed for her to get out of there, then gave her a shove to shake her out of the shock.

He came up for air as another bullet hit the water near the log by his head. Blair reached for him. "Come on! Hurry." She'd made it to waist-deep water and was crouching behind a fallen tree.

Holt couldn't leave Bryan like that. He had to do something.

Another shot.

There was nothing he could do for his friend. But he could save Blair. He'd promised. He made it to her, snatched his gun and covered her. "Run! For the trees! Go!"

Blair sprinted through the forest, twigs cracking underneath her bare feet. She must have lost her flip-flops in the water. Her feet were going to be cut up. If he could carry her and not get her killed he would.

Another *crack* sounded.

Fire split through Holt's shoulder.

He'd been hit.

Blair raced through the trees, branches reaching out like claws scratching her arms. She jumped logs and ignored the stinging on the bottom of her feet. They had to get to safety. Who was that floating in the water? Instinct told her whoever was after Blair had put him there. And by the looks of it, he'd been there awhile. Blair's stomach roiled and she tried to shove the image from her mind. *Keep running. Just run. Lord, help us!*

Holt grunted and Blair pivoted. Blood seeped down his left shoulder. "You've been shot!" She flew to him, but he shook his head. "Go! I'm fine. Keep running. I'm right behind you. Promise."

Blair hesitated but continued on. If her direction was right they'd end up on Mitch Rydell's property and near his stables. She only hoped whoever was out there didn't have a keen sense of direction. Heart thumping in her chest, she glanced back. Holt was right behind her, gun in hand, scanning the woods as he went.

Protecting her.

No one was protecting him.

It hit her like an anvil.

The shots had pelted above his head. Where he was located in the water.

They'd hit him.

They weren't aiming for Blair. They were targeting Holt. Making good on their threat and coming after the people Blair cared about. Whether she liked it or not, Holt was on that list, rising to the top with every conversation.

He'd opened up about his painful past. If that wasn't honesty, what was?

He'd almost kissed her. Again.

She darted left.

Someone fired and bark from a tree exploded above Holt's head.

"Keep going, Blair." He fired a shot in the direction of the assailant.

In the distance, Mitch's stables came into view. Shelter. But first she'd have to make it through the clearing. About fifty feet. Surely, someone wouldn't shoot in the open like that. But the attackers knew the police were now involved—except they weren't really—and they might feel like they had nothing to lose.

Blair whispered a prayer for safety for her and Holt and urged her legs farther and faster, her calves burning and her feet nearly coming out from under her.

Holt was right on her heels.

A stable hand stepped into Blair's line of sight and she flagged him down, praying they were in the clear.

He hollered and another man, and Mitch, came out of the stables.

"Mitch! Call Doc Drummond. Holt's been shot," Blair hollered.

The man with Mitch grabbed his phone. Mitch ran to Blair and Holt, his hat flying off in the breeze. "How did this happen?"

Holt skidded to a stop next to Blair, his clothes soaking wet and blood streaking down his arm. He raised his shirtsleeve. "I think…I think maybe some kids were goofing off in the woods. Just a graze."

"We're back to kids and pranks?" Mitch grunted. "Come on in the house and we'll wait for Doc to get here."

Blair had never been inside Mitch's home, only his stables. A big brick two-story with a wraparound porch.

A large kitchen full of windows giving him an incredible view of rolling pastures and his horses. Everything was stainless steel, hardwood and tasteful but masculine. She and Holt dripped on his tiled floor. "Have a seat. I'll get ya'll a glass of water and towels." He disappeared from the kitchen. Holt slumped in a chair, his free hand holding his head. Seeing that body must have done a number on him, too.

This was all Blair's fault. If she'd never dragged Holt into this, he wouldn't have gotten shot, even if it was a flesh wound. But she'd allowed him in and let herself care about him, more than she ever meant to. Once again her choices had hurt someone.

"I'm so sorry, Holt. I'm responsible for this."

He raised his head, his eyes smoldering with a quiet fury that sent a shiver into her bones. "You are not responsible for that. Not for this." He pointed to his shoulder. "And for…for that body." His voice cracked and he hung his head again.

"I don't know who that was in the water. No one has been missing in town. But we're going to have to call Beckett. We can't let a man stay there that way. It isn't right. He might have a family." Blair wiped her eyes.

Holt nodded but didn't speak.

Mitch came in with a few towels. He walked to the fridge and snagged two bottles of water and set them on the table. Blair opened Holt's, then her own and took a long drink. Her throat and lungs still burned.

"Looks like you went for a dip in the lake."

"How long do you think till Doc Drummond gets here?" Holt asked.

"He lives on the other side of my property. Ten minutes if he's…" Mitch glanced outside. An ATV was cutting across his lawn, its humming motor bringing all their attention to the window. "He's here."

Doc Drummond grabbed a bag and swung off the ATV before heading into the house. Mitch pointed to Holt.

"What happened?" Doc Drummond set his medical bag down and removed a pair of scissors, cutting away Holt's shirt.

Now was not the time to take in more of Holt's flawlessness. Or inspect the interesting display of tattoos on his shoulder, biceps and side.

Holt remained silent. Was he in shock? Blair spoke up. "He was grazed by a bullet in the woods."

Mitch glared and shook his head. "I'm calling Beckett."

Blair squeezed her eyes shut. No point in arguing. It was the right thing to do. Besides, there was a body in the lake that needed to be attended to. Doc Drummond worked on Holt's arm. "You're right. Only a graze." He bent him forward, looked at his shoulder and frowned.

"What's the matter?" Blair asked.

Doc Drummond continued to inspect Holt's other shoulder.

"Nothing," Doc Drummond said. "Just being thorough."

Blair wasn't so sure. Seemed he'd found something awfully interesting there.

Holt inhaled but said nothing; his nostrils worked in and out and his jaw clenched. After he was patched up, Mitch brought him a fresh T-shirt.

"Thanks," Holt said, and worked his way into it without so much as wince. "Where's the bathroom?"

Mitch pointed off the kitchen. Holt practically sprinted inside. This had to be dreadful for him. Saving her from a snake was one thing, but now he was getting shot at and finding dead bodies. Even if he said it wasn't her fault, his actions proved he was torn up and beside himself.

"You hurt, Blair?" Doc Drummond asked.

"Some scratches on my feet and arms. Mostly shaken up, I guess. Thank you for coming so quickly."

He took her feet and began cleaning her up. She winced.

"I was just relaxing by the pool with Riella. We've been swamped lately. I'm sure she'll offer Sophia's enchiladas again. It's her specialty."

Blair smirked. "Riella's or Sophia's?"

"Both." He chuckled and the doorbell rang.

Mitch strode to the front and then Beckett Marsh followed him into the kitchen. "Am I wasting my time today?" His maple-colored eyes bored into Blair's.

Blair sighed. "I don't know who was shooting at us or why. But there is something you should know. There's a man's body in the lake. On the western edge in Lovers' Cove."

Mitch raised his eyebrows and Blair frowned. They hadn't been there on purpose. Holt had no idea that couples went there for romantic moments. "By the logs, about fifteen feet from the bank. My foot got tangled in a rope. It was…" She shivered. "Holding him down." She covered her face, and Mitch sat beside her and slung his arm around her.

Beckett got on his radio and called it in. Wouldn't be long before a crowd of people surrounded the area as they drew the body out. "Anything else you want to confess?"

"No."

Holt came from the bathroom, his expression torn.

Beckett gave him a once-over. "You clipped?"

"Flesh wound," Doc Drummond said.

Holt glanced at his shoulder. "I'm good."

"I told him about the man we found in the lake. He's sending his team out now."

Holt's jaw hardened. "I have nothing to add."

Beckett grunted. "Didn't figure you would, Renard. Seems like a lot of trouble has come to my town since you arrived."

"Are you implying something, Deputy Chief?" Holt

countered, menace lacing his voice. Now was not the time for these two to pick a fight. And none of this had to do with Holt. He was an innocent bystander who'd been at the wrong place at the wrong time the day Blair was attacked on Farley Pass.

Blair stood. "We've told you everything we know, Beckett. We…we need to rest. Process." She handed Mitch her towel and finger-combed her knotted hair. "We appreciate the help." Turning to Doc, she said, "And thank you. For everything."

"Seems like I'm putting you or someone close to you back together often." He smirked. "Don't be surprised if Riella shows up with *several* dishes of enchiladas."

She mustered a smile. "I'll consider myself warned, then."

Beckett swiped a hand over his square jaw. "I'm going to have follow-up questions. Right now I need to get to Hope Lake and see if we can figure out who's out there and why." He started to leave and doubled back, resting his hands on Blair's shoulders. "I'm sorry you had to find him, to see that. I'm not your enemy, Blair."

Blair nodded. Beckett was only trying to do his job. One that Blair bucked at every turn. He wasn't an idiot. He knew something sinister was going on.

He acknowledged Holt with a tip of his chin and let himself out.

"Thanks for fixing me up, Doc." Holt gave Mitch back the wet towel and hung on to the bloody one. "I guess I owe you a towel."

"No worries. Glad you're in one piece," Mitch said. "Blair, holler if you need anything. Manny'll drive ya'll home. Or back to the lake for your vehicle. Whichever you want." He walked them to the front door.

They chose to return to the lake for Holt's truck. He kept silent on the way home. Pulling into her drive, he inhaled. "I, uh… I'm tired, Blair. I'm gonna go to my place and rest. But if you need anything, come get me. Or call. I'll bunk on the couch later."

She didn't want to be alone, but Blair couldn't blame him from wanting his distance from her. She'd almost gotten him killed. "If that's what you want. Again, I'm sorry, Holt. More than you can imagine."

She hurried out of the truck and up the walkway.

She had a sinking feeling that any chance of a budding romance with Holt had met the same fate as the man in the lake.

EIGHT

Four days had passed since Holt discovered Bryan Livingston's body. He'd felt like a heel leaving Blair alone after the horrible event, but he needed to be alone for a while, and deal with the fact that he'd been too late. He hadn't saved Bryan. Not to mention he had follow-up work to do that had to stay private. He'd wanted to come clean with her, but he'd been instructed not to reveal his identity. His mission wasn't over yet.

Now that Bryan was dead, Holt worried Jeremy might be, too. Hope had taxied its way into the stratosphere of Holt's heart only to crash and burn when they'd discovered Bryan. His friend left behind a wife and two children.

Life could be so unfair.

So much less than wonderful, which was how he felt, lying to Blair. Yet the thought of telling her the truth scared him to death. Holt had continued to spend the last few nights on Blair's couch, keeping watch over her and Gigi. But he'd come in late and left early. The struggle to look Blair in the eye worsened with each second, so he simply avoided her.

He was to blame for whatever might have happened to Jeremy. It didn't matter that Holt had warned him not to poke around or eavesdrop too much. He'd allowed him to take that job at the trucking company, knowing the risks.

Holt had been taking risks since Trina died.

He didn't care if he lived or died.

But Jeremy did care.

What if he couldn't save Jeremy?

Even if he could bring down this cartel and bring justice for Bryan and Jeremy, and convince Blair that he'd been bound by his job to lie about his identity, she would never forgive him for using Jeremy as his informant or allowing him to go into a hazardous situation. She wouldn't care that he'd been honest about his feelings for her and the past experiences he'd shared. And he didn't blame her. He would never forgive himself, either.

Holt took a few cleansing breaths and ambled down the cobblestone walk toward Sufficient Grounds. Deputy Chief Marsh was parked on the street next to the Read It and Steep tea shop, deep in conversation with the owner. Holt wasn't sure what to make of Beckett Marsh. The man was too smart. Too intuitive. He might not be the murderer or behind the attacks, but that didn't mean he wasn't in the Juarez Cartel's pocket, and until Holt knew for sure if he could be trusted, he'd work the investigation here on his own and let his colleagues at the DEA work the other end.

For now he'd pretend he had no idea who Bryan Livingston was. Of course, it wouldn't be long before Beckett had the dental record answers and would know exactly who Bryan was. Still, Holt had been instructed to play dumb as long as he was uncertain which side Beckett Marsh was on.

For a moment Holt had believed God wasn't cruel after all. Now he was back to thinking He might be. Or at the very least, uninterested in good winning over evil. The bad guys were winning all too often.

He planned to sit inside Sufficient Grounds with a cup of coffee and listen for gossip surrounding the events, and in general, hoped to glean a lead or a nugget of information that would prove useful. Best way to learn about people was to eavesdrop.

Beckett Marsh got out of his car and approached Holt at the door to the coffee shop. "Renard. How's it going?"

"It's going. Any news on that guy in the lake?"

"No identification. Couldn't get prints on him. He'd been in the water awhile..." He grimaced. "Well, we just couldn't."

Holt's stomach turned. Someone would pay for what happened to Bryan. "Dental records?" How far into the investigation was he?

"Working on that now." Marsh folded his arms across his chest. "I saw Blair this morning. She looked worse for the wear. I'm worried about her."

Holt ground his teeth together. "That makes two of us."

"Talked to Hunter Black at the bait shop yesterday. Says Gigi told him her brother's been AWOL for a few weeks." Marsh cocked his head, a penetrating gleam in his eye.

"What's that have to do with me?" If Beckett was so concerned, he should do a background check on Holt. He'd find a solid cover story to show he was an upstanding citizen. Not even a parking ticket, thanks to the computer analysts at the DEA.

"I guess nothing." He continued to eye Holt. "Seems odd is all. Brother missing. Blair looking like walking death. Guns. Dead bodies. Businesses broken into." He shrugged. "I'll be real interested to see who our John Doe is. Should be another day or so before we find out."

Hearing Bryan called John Doe made Holt squirm.

"I did a check on the brother. Trying to give the Sullivan girls some peace of mind. He's had a few run-ins with the law over drugs. I can't help wondering if he brought some kind of trouble to his sisters."

"I doubt that."

"Why?" Marsh raised an eyebrow. "You don't even know Jeremy Sullivan. Do you?"

"I'm done here." Holt brushed past him, not bothering to be gentle when he bumped his shoulder. Beckett Marsh acted like he might know more about Holt than he let on. Or more about the situation. Antagonizing another law enforcer wasn't Holt's typical behavior, but he was on edge. Not the best way to make friends, like Mitch Rydell said. Mitch. He had a close watch on Blair's house. Her barn. Pretty rich guy. All from horses? Possible. Or maybe he was dabbling with drug trafficking. Someone from the trade was embedded deep here, careful not to stand out.

Inside the coffee shop, he scanned the seating area. Bistro tables in the middle were full. Teenagers drinking coffee, thinking they were all grown up. A young bubbly girl and a high school boy stood behind the counter taking orders and laughing with customers.

Holt stood in line, ears peeled to conversations going on around him. In the corner next to the door, Lola Medina, who owned the boutique next to the defense attorney's office, caught his eye. Everything had come back clean on her; no connection to drugs or cartels could be found, but that only meant if she was tied to a cartel, and her trip overseas had been to meet with someone involved, they'd all been careful. Holt needed answers. Now. While Lola was here sipping coffee, he could poke around her home, the boutique.

He walked outside and smacked right into Blair.

Beckett Marsh's words came to mind. She looked like walking death.

"Long time no see," he said, keeping it light. Awkward tension flowed between them.

"Any news on Jeremy?" she asked.

The dark circles under Blair's eyes and her ashen skin

sent him into despair. He had no words. He refused to give her false promises like the ones he'd given Trina. "No."

"Okay, thanks," she murmured, and tried to scoot past him. She must think he was fickle. Almost kissing her at the lake and then avoiding her like the plague. Or she might think he was angry with her because he'd been shot. He'd been shot before in the line of duty. Doc Drummond had probably suspected as much by the way he'd examined his shoulder.

Holt blocked her path to the door. "I'm sorry for being scarce lately." He had a job to do and guilt to suppress.

She replied with a weak smile.

"I am." If she only knew how sorry. "You look like you haven't slept."

"I haven't. I can't quit thinking about Jeremy." She heaved a sigh. "And every time I close my eyes I see that snake or feel someone in the room, even when I'm alone."

Even with him on her couch, she wasn't sleeping. She didn't think he could protect her after all. And maybe he couldn't.

"I don't blame you for avoiding me. It's my fault what happened. I'm thinking of telling Beckett the truth. I might need law enforcement on my side after all. I mean, I know I've needed it. Seems like it doesn't matter if they know or not. I was heading over to the station after I got a cup of coffee. To come clean. And you won't have to sleep on my couch anymore."

"I don't mind sleeping on your couch. I'm there because I want to be. And me getting shot is no one's fault but the shooter's." Going to Beckett was a bad idea, but how could Holt steer her away from it? If Beckett was connected, why would the note tell her not to go to the police? Unless they planned to test her with each interrogation.

"Well, I'm sorry anyway."

A rock settled in his gut. "No. I'm sorry." For lying. Deceiving. Withholding information. And not being enough to make her feel safe.

"Don't be. You didn't do anything but help." A little light came back into her eyes. "I do appreciate you sleeping on the couch. The bit of sleep I do get is because I know you're there."

Holt laced his hand in hers. "Good. I just needed some time. After seeing the victim in the lake. It's not you. It has nothing to do with you."

She nodded. "It's okay, I understand. There's something I've been wanting to tell you, too. I couldn't dodge my dad's questions anymore and I refused to outright lie to him. He knows Jeremy is missing. He's flying home and in the meantime sent an old marine buddy to search crack houses in Memphis. But nothing has turned up."

"Does he know about what's been going on here?"

She shook her head. "No, the less anyone knows, the better off they'll be. I don't want my dad hurt. I don't want anyone in this town hurt…because of me. I love this place."

Holt was quickly becoming attached to Hope, too. But this wasn't his life. He couldn't stay. "I agree with that. You have to do what you think is best to keep people you care about safe."

"They're having a cookout in the square tonight. Would you like to go?" Blair asked. "Casually. It's not a date or anything." Her nervous laugh undid him.

"What time?" He had some investigating to do.

"It's at seven. But games are going on at five. Horseshoes, croquet, badminton."

"I'm a badminton champ, so count me in."

He agreed to go, not because it would be a great place to mingle and listen, but because he wanted every minute he could grab with this woman. Before she hated him for life.

* * *

"I sold at least three hundred dollars' worth of stuff today. I rock the retail. You just missed Hunter. I even talked him into a few purchases." Gigi swung her legs as she sat on the counter. "Hey, you all right?"

Blair wasn't sure she was. Jeremy was still missing without a trace. They weren't sure who the man in the water was. Holt's distance had her dazed. But today he'd seemed almost normal. She'd missed him terribly, even if he was bunking on her couch. They'd been growing closer each day until the shoot-out. And whoever was after her was lurking in wait. Which was almost as bad as coming out with a full-fledged assault. She stayed on pins and needles.

"I'm just worried." She had gone to the station to talk to Beckett but changed her mind because it would end in her spilling her guts about her past. Embarrassment won out. And really, what more could he do that he wasn't doing anyway?

"We're all worried. Talk's all over the town about that man in the lake. Hunter said some people say he was in the Mafia. Aurora Daniels has been to the police station every day inquiring about him. Weird, huh?"

That was strange. Why would Aurora care about a man she couldn't even defend? "Are you going to the Dinner on the Square? With Hunter?"

Gigi groaned. "Yes. I guess."

"You guess? I thought you were on again. He was just here. What's the deal?"

"He has commitment issues. Doesn't want to end up divorced like his parents." Gigi jumped off the counter. "I want him to make a choice already."

"Hasty decisions can end in disaster. I'm a case in point."

The bell jingled and an older man stepped inside.

Slicked-back midnight hair pulled away from his high brow. Dark, narrowed eyes with crags around the lids focused on her. Maybe in his younger years he'd have been attractive. Now his presence was…unnerving. "Ladies." He tipped his straw fedora and perused the shelves.

"Are you looking for something in particular?" Blair asked, and rubbed the goose bumps forming on her arms.

"I'm a collector of hand-carved items. I heard there was quite an assortment of crafts here."

Gigi wandered his way. Blair wanted to grab her back, but she was already next to the man with a heavy Latino accent. "Where are you visiting from?" Gigi asked.

"I have family in town."

"Oh, who?" Gigi asked. Talk about small-town nosiness. Gigi had adopted it well. But Blair had ice running through her veins.

He smiled, ignored her question.

"Gigi, can you do me a favor and head on home? I need that frozen casserole in the oven on three-fifty for an hour, and I still need to do a few things here." Best thing was to get her sister out. Better safe than sorry.

"Yeah." She frowned. "Sure."

She waited until Gigi was out the door, then turned on the man. "I do have a display of hand-carved items. Mostly they're over there." She pointed to the section by the front door. Swallowing, she gripped her cell phone. "I didn't catch your name."

"I didn't give it, senora." A sinister smile spread across his severe face, and he touched several items. Picking them up, studying them. "How do you come across all these fascinating trinkets?"

Blair willed her pulse to slow down. Now would be a great time for Holt to come in. Or Beckett Marsh. "Oh, I go to auctions, wholesale retailers, mom-and-pop places."

He toyed with a wooden car, then placed it back on the shelf. "You remind me of someone."

"I do?" she squeaked.

"Mmm… Are you married?"

A lump was lodged in her throat as this man seemed to slither toward her. The coral snake in her bed came to mind. Was this man poisonous, too? "I'm widowed, actually."

"That's too bad." He placed a wooden cigar box on the counter. "I'll take this. I'm a fan of Colombian cigars. I have a little shop in Bogotá. Ever been there? Maybe you bought this there?"

Blood drained from her head, and her knees turned to water. Mateo was killed in Bogotá. And yes, she had several cigar boxes from all over the world. Mateo had collected them. She didn't answer, couldn't, her throat was as scratchy as sandpaper.

Hands trembling, she wrapped the box in butcher paper.

"I was having coffee earlier. Heard about a man who drowned in the lake. Such an unfortunate tragedy."

She shoved the box in the paper bag. "Yes, it's terrible," she whispered. "That'll be fifteen dollars and sixty-two cents."

He meticulously counted out the money, and then he placed it in her hand and squeezed it into her palm. "Tragedies happen all the time. Unfortunate accidents. Accidents that could be avoided." He released her hand. "You sure I don't know you? You look very much like the wife of a man I once knew. His life ended tragically, as well."

Blair found her voice. "I think I'd remember meeting you."

"Lovely girl, that sister of yours," he said, his voice gravelly. "Enjoy your day, Mrs. Salvador." He slinked out of the shop and Blair rushed to the front door, locking it.

This had nothing to do with Jeremy. This had everything to do with Mateo and his enemies.

A knock on the window sent her leaping in the air and shrieking. She turned and saw Holt twisting the knob. "Blair, let me in!"

She fumbled with the locks and opened the door. "He was here."

"Who was here?"

"A man. The dead man in the lake—he was involved with drugs. And they killed him. He knows Mateo. He's—he's here!"

Holt's eyes widened, then hardened. "What was his name?"

"He didn't give it." Her heart raced until she thought it might explode. "Not quite six foot. Latino. Major accent. Older. Maybe early fifties? He wore a gold pinky ring with a red jewel in it."

Holt's jaw clenched along with his fist. "Did he threaten you? Tell me everything."

Blair spat out what had happened from beginning to end.

"Where's Gigi?" Holt asked.

"I sent her home for the casserole. I should go to her. Now. Make sure he didn't do anything." She bent behind the counter for her purse and keys.

Holt sorted through the section the man had been perusing. "Do you think he stole anything?"

"I don't think so. I think he wanted to let me know he…he had a hand in Mateo's death. He knew he collected those boxes. Knew he was murdered in Bogotá." She fumbled through her purse. "Where are my keys?"

Holt crossed to the counter. "Calm down. We'll find them."

Gigi stormed into the store area. Blair gaped.

"Yeah. As if I didn't know you were trying to get rid of me. You're keeping things from me again. You promised!"

"I'm not," Blair insisted. "I haven't had time to tell you anything. But you can't be wandering around alone."

"We have to do something. Call Beckett. Call the... I don't know... Call the National Guard. Or the DEA. Bring those jokers in. I mean, isn't it their job to deal with drug cartels? How do you even go about doing that?" Gigi flailed her arms and paced between the aisles of merchandise.

Holt massaged the back of his neck. "Let's be rational. Dental records will give authorities the identity of the man from the lake. At that point they'll start investigating. Find out where this man is from, what he did for a living, and perhaps then they'll make a connection to the man who was here today."

"But this creepy guy is in town now. We should send Beckett to find out who he is and where he's staying." Gigi crossed her arms over her chest, glared at Blair for backup.

Blair slumped on a velvet high-back chair. "Beckett can't win. Not against this man. If he's cartel, he's high up and ruthless. We'd find Beckett at the bottom of a lake." She shook her head. "He's safer not knowing anything."

Holt seemed once again torn as he ate up the wooden floor, matching Gigi stride for stride as they paced, but he kept quiet.

"Then we need someone equally ruthless and powerful," Gigi said.

Blair glanced at Gigi. Holt froze.

"We call Hector." Gigi threw her arms out. "He considers you family, right? So call and tell him that someone who had connections to Mateo's death is here in Hope flaunting it and has threatened you and me. He'll come and save us."

"Absolutely not!" Holt roared.

Blair jumped at the force behind his voice. Gigi crunched on her bottom lip. "It was just a thought, Holt."

"You cannot call a drug lord to come in. You'll incite a war. There will be casualties. You'll both end up dead."

"And we'll be indebted to Hector. I can't owe him, Gigi. You don't understand the danger here." Blair would never admit it had crossed her mind. Holt could only protect her for so long before she got him killed.

"Fine. We'll sit around while they keep scaring us half to death over who knows what! What do they want? They've never even said." Gigi charged out the back entrance.

"She can't traipse off alone," Blair said.

"I'll go get her. Don't move from this spot." Holt's authoritative voice scared and impressed her. He was right—bringing Hector here would incite a war. But calling in anyone else was out of the question. Gigi had a point, too. The cartel members were looking for something.

It was like they assumed Blair knew what it was. And how to give it back. She'd been through the log and the inventory. She had nothing. What if they had retrieved it and these new attacks were threats to keep her mouth shut?

How long would they ensue?

Probably as long as Beckett investigated on his own. Blair didn't know how to make Beckett stop without revealing the truth, and even then, he wouldn't. He would do his job.

Holt stormed inside. "Hunter met her in the parking lot. They're going back to his place. He knows everything, by the way. She's told him."

Blair heaved a sigh. "I guess I can't blame her. She loves him. Says a lot that he came. Even if he does have commitment issues."

Holt strode to the window, scanning the area. "It puts him in danger."

"I put you in danger."

"That's different. I inserted myself."

Right. Blair hadn't invited him into her problems. But she was grateful he was here. And…and if she was honest with herself she'd admit she was falling in love with him even though she'd been working not to. Didn't mean he was feeling the same way. "Why do you keep putting yourself in danger? I know why Hunter's willing to do it."

Holt faced her. His eyes dimmed and his mouth drooped. "I care about you."

Then why look so sad about it?

He cared about her. Just the words she wanted to hear. Not. Silence filled the room in a most uncomfortable way. "So, what now?"

Holt slicked his hands over his face. "Have you thought about leaving town for a while?"

NINE

"It's Alejandro," Holt said. "The description fit him to a tee. Even the pinky ring with the ruby. He's here. I have to act fast." Holt paced his living room, glancing out the window to the opposite side of the street. The best thing was to go to the cookout on the square. Maybe he'd find something suspicious. It was still hard to believe that Alejandro Gonzalez had been one store away from him. Threatening Blair, no less.

Holt's handler, Drake Billington, sighed over the line. "If you do find Alejandro, you can't do anything rash. We need him to lead us to Juarez. He won't flip. We can't arrest him."

Holt gripped the phone so tight he feared he would crush it. "But he threatened Blair. I think I should tell her the truth."

"This mission isn't about Blair Sullivan, Holt. The answer is no. You know if you fraternize with an asset, you'll be relieved of your duties. This isn't some cop show or movie. There are consequences for such an action. You want to ruin your career over one woman?"

Law enforcement hadn't been Holt's first choice, but he had made a career out of it. A good one. It kept him moving and busy.

"Do you hear me, Holt?"

"Loud and clear." His gut ached.

"This mission is about finding who Alejandro was meeting with. About bringing down the head of the Juarez Cartel and bringing justice to Agent Bryan Livingston. Our friend. And finding Jeremy Sullivan."

Holt growled. "And what if Alejandro attempts to hurt Blair? Am I supposed to let him?"

"Stop acting irrational and get your head on straight. You know that's not what I mean."

Holt's frustration brewed hot and dangerous. "I'm alone here. Hitting dead ends at every turn. I'm convinced there was something in that storage unit. Did you find out who owns it?"

"A corporation. Hollow Chest. Looks legit, but it's possible the Juarez Cartel is using it to funnel money and drugs. Maybe even trafficking. We're trying to establish connections between the corporation and anyone in the cartel. Without Jeremy's intel, we have nothing for a warrant."

"We have to have more than that. Any connections to Jeremy, drugs and the cartel?"

"Keith Hill. Over-the-road truck driver at the same terminal Jeremy worked. Runs Memphis to Texas. But so do four other guys. We're still checking. No direct links to any Juarez Cartel members, but he has a few drug possession charges from his early twenties."

"Maybe Jeremy found information through him, or on him." Holt stared out the window.

"Possible. Can't connect him to the cartel, though. That's our issue. And it's why we can't get a warrant to search a single thing on him."

"What about Beckett Marsh? I don't like him."

"Well, that must be a case of two alpha males butting heads. He's clean."

"Doesn't mean he's clean."

Drake chuckled. "No, but he's a former SEAL. Part of his record is classified. He's even received a few awards. Rumor has it he was offered a job in the Secret Service. Turned it down to come back home."

"Shut up." Who would turn down that kind of action for a small-town life? He wasn't even in charge. Blair stepped out onto the porch, and Holt's heart skittered.

A woman. That would flip a man's plan on a dime. Holt was even considering it, which was ridiculous. Blair would have nothing to do with him when she found out the truth. The lying was starting to seriously kill him, though.

"I'm not kidding. I don't think he's in cahoots. Your call if you want to fill him in. You said you're alone. Maybe you're not. Dental records are in. He knows about Bryan. You're the one there, so use your judgment. But keep your cover to Blair Sullivan. Understood?"

"Got it." He hung up. Beckett Marsh, Navy SEAL. Maybe Holt could use him after all. If the storage unit facility was a cover to traffic money and drugs, why auction it off? No one could be certain who would purchase it. Unless the wrong unit was auctioned off by accident. Or drugs were placed in the wrong unit. There was no other explanation.

Holt met Blair in his yard. She wore a navy blue dress with a billowy skirt that blew in the breeze. She'd left her hair down, his favorite style. Straight and nearly touching her waist. "You thought anymore about what I said earlier? About getting out of town?"

"No way. This is my home. I'm not leaving it. I don't want trouble. But trouble already came. If I leave they'll follow me. I'll always have to run."

Holt nodded. He couldn't lose her.

He loved her.

There it was. The words. The truth.

A love he'd never experienced before. A mature love. Deep. Abiding. More powerful than he could hardly stand.

"Holt?" Blair frowned. "What's wrong? You have a weird look on your face. Has something happened?"

"Yes." His voice turned husky. He cupped her cheek and ran a thumb across her bottom lip. "I don't want to lose you, Blair."

Her breath hitched, and he didn't give her time to respond with words as his lips descended on hers.

Easy. Tender. Slow.

Years of hope, packed down tight, suddenly unearthed. New dreams stirred. A few old dreams wiggled free.

Blair wrapped her arms around his neck and hung on as if she feared he might let go. The only way he would is if she pushed him away when he *was* able to reveal the truth.

And she would.

But right now Holt needed to share this moment. To reveal his heart. Nothing in this kiss lied. It was as pure as a bubbling brook, as fresh-fallen snow. Nothing hidden. No deceit.

And she wasn't hiding hers, either. She matched his intensity with a fervor all her own. A kiss like this... Maybe they could find their way to stay together, to find forgiveness.

But if not, he would at least have this one true moment when their hearts had been laid bare. When they'd held nothing back. Like a wave that rose and rode its way onto the shore, lapping a few moments before ebbing back into the sea. He broke it off before it swelled again.

Blair's eyes remained closed, a rosy glow dusted her cheeks, a smirk played on her semiswollen lips. "Flawless," she breathed. "I knew it would be."

He leaned down, pecked her on the lips, then nuzzled

his nose against hers. "That better be the only flawless kiss you've ever had in this town. In this lifetime, now that I think about it." One last kiss to her forehead and he laced his fingers with hers. "This is where you say it is the only flawless kiss you've had."

She leaned into his upper arm, not quite tall enough to lay her head on his shoulder. "You have no reason to feel insecure."

He chuckled. "I'm taking that as a yes."

"I'm not sure if that's true." Mischief played in her eyes. "You've only kissed me once."

He walked her to the truck, then swept her up and kissed her again until he couldn't breathe. Setting her down, he righted her when she stumbled, and held in his laughter. His insides were doing the same thing. All equilibrium in his heart was gone.

"Ready?"

"You can't keep doing that, ya know?" She sighed and strapped on her seat belt.

Unfortunately, he did know. But he refused to allow guilt to ruin this evening. He kissed her hand, then closed her door.

Tonight he was stealing the chance to be a man in love with a woman who *had* to be in love with him. He'd felt it. In her kiss.

So long, eighty-degree temps. Hello, high nineties. Yet Blair stood in line for her hazelnut blend coffee with a shot of espresso. She'd barely slept last night. Partly because of the man showing up in her store, partly because the night had been lovely. Full moon. The smells of the South smothered in grease and tangy sauces. She and Holt had listened to the worship band near the gazebo while watching kids play with water balloons. Men had laughed over a friendly game of horseshoes. Even Holt had joined in after his third dessert. He'd mentioned something about small towns ruining his health regimen. Hadn't stopped him from taking that last bite of strawberry cake with cream-cheese icing.

She placed her order and carried her coffee outside to the corner that looked out near the courthouse. Last night had been almost perfect. Holt had slept on the couch, but they'd gone home. Together. Had she been playing one of her rounds of pretend? Had he?

That kiss had said otherwise.

That incredible, amazing kiss that had sent her into a state of blissful vertigo had to have meant something. It had to her. Holt had busted through her barricade and opened her up to trust. And with her trust and vulnerability came her ability to fall in love.

And she had done exactly that. More than anything, she wanted to bask in it. Go wild with it. But Hector's enemy was in town and wanted her dead.

"You off in la-la land?" Ronnie Lawson straightened his VOLS cap and plopped onto the sidewalk next to Blair, a cup of coffee and a Danish in hand.

"It was enjoyable, too. You driving out to Arlington for the July estate sale? Looks like a big one." She sipped her nutty brew.

"Thinking about it." He motioned his chin in the direction of It's A Wonderful Life. "You not opening up shop today?"

Blair frowned and glanced at the time on her cell phone. "What do you mean? Gigi opened over two hours ago." She'd heard her leave.

"Well, it's dark as night up in there. Locked tight, too."

Throat turning raw, Blair rifled through her purse and grabbed her phone. She punched Gigi's name and prayed she answered.

"Everything all right?" Ronnie stood, staring.

Voice mail. She tried the store. The recording kicked on.

Maybe she was with Hunter. "I'm fine, Ronnie. I—I gotta go." She jumped up, sprinting toward the Black-Eyed Pea as Hunter's phone went to voice mail, too.

Her blood chilled.

She burst through the door, causing a few customers to glance at her.

Calm down, Blair. Don't cause a scene.

She rushed to the counter, willing herself to keep her composure. Jace breezed through the kitchen in his gray V-neck T-shirt, his hair pulled back in a short but messy man bun. Some of his wavy bangs hung around his eyes.

"Hey, you seen Hunter?" he asked.

Blair's heart sputtered and she nearly choked. "I was coming to find G. Have you seen her this morning?"

"Nope. Not since last night around eleven, when I heard Hunter's truck rumbling. Assumed he was taking her home." Jace grabbed the white towel hanging off his shoulder and wiped down the counter. "You see 'em, tell him to get his lazy bum over here. I'm shorthanded."

Should she worry Jace? One more person Blair had put in the crosshairs. "Sure thing."

Blair rushed from the diner and weaved between pedestrians. A few hollered greetings and made jokes about her being in a hurry. She shoved open Holt's door, huffing and puffing.

"Gigi and Hunter...they're missing."

Holt jumped over the half swinging door separating the shopping floor from the counter area. "How do you know?"

"She didn't open up the store. Ronnie Lawson just told me she wasn't there." Blair's entire body had turned cold. "She's not answering her phone, and neither is Hunter."

Holt snatched his keys. "Then let's take a trip to Hunter's." He locked the door and they climbed in his truck.

"He lives in the apartment above Jace's garage. Over on Lindenberry. Near the Magnolia Inn."

Holt nodded and laid on the gas. "Try her phone again."

Blair tried one more time. "Nothing."

Holt turned onto Magnolia Lane, past the inn Mrs. McKay owned and ran. As he turned on Lindenberry, Gigi's blue Jeep Wrangler came into view. Hunter's black truck was also in the drive.

"They're here."

Blair laid a hand on her chest and breathed deep. "Good. Good. I'm going to kill her."

Holt took the stairs ahead of her and stopped at the door. "Go back downstairs. Now."

Blair tried to push past Holt, but he was like Mt. Everest. "What? Why?"

"The door's partly opened." He drew his gun and put his finger on his lips. "I'm going in," he whispered. "You go back down those stairs. Get in the driver's side and be ready to go straight to Beckett Marsh if I'm not out in five minutes."

"No," Blair protested. Her sister might be in there. Might be... No, she refused to consider it.

"Blair Sullivan. I appreciate your mind and that you speak it often. But right now I'm not gonna tell you again. Get. Down. Those. Stairs." His eyes held steel, his voice low but full of ultimate authority.

She nodded, sucked her lip in to hold back sobs and headed to Holt's truck, climbing inside. Holt nodded at her, then used his foot to swing the door open. He slipped inside, and lights flashed behind her. Beckett Marsh barreled into the driveway.

Who called him?

* * *

Holt didn't need but one foot in the door to know the place had been trashed. The living room opened into the kitchen. CDs, books and hunting magazines littered the floor. Holt spotted a bedroom to the left. He kept his gun out, in case the intruder was still here. He cleared the small bathroom. Untouched.

Toeing open the bedroom door, he came to a halt. Gigi. Tied up. He shoved his gun inside his waistband and removed the bandanna from her mouth. "Hunter! Where's Hunter?"

Holt's stomach somersaulted as he untied Gigi from the desk chair. "How long have you been like this?" The ropes had cut into Gigi's wrists. Mascara streamed her cheeks. He worked on untying her ankles from the chair legs.

She fell into him, sobbing, her arms draped around his neck. "Hunter went to take the trash out. I thought it was him coming inside. But it wasn't."

"Did you see who it was? One person? Two?" Holt tipped her chin. "Did he hurt you, Gigi?" He scanned her clothes. They didn't appear torn or disheveled.

She shook her head. "I jumped up when he came in. I don't know who he was. He wore a ski mask. He came at me and before I knew it, I was tied to this stupid chair. I couldn't even call out for Hunter." She hiccupped through her weeping. "Did you find him? Did he call you?"

"We'll find him." He couldn't promise in what kind of condition. "What time was this?"

"Before seven this morning. His truck was messed up, so I came by to take him to work and he made us breakfast."

The front door squeaked.

Holt drew his weapon. That had better not be Blair. He signaled for Gigi to remain quiet and skulked to the bedroom door.

Holt used his first two fingers, pointed at Gigi, then motioned for her to enter the closet. She nodded, her body trembling as she crept across the room.

Holt kept his back against wall, waiting.

A creak sounded in a floor joist by the bedroom door. Silence.

A shadow emerged.

Holt slid around the door, his gun aimed on the intruder.

The intruder aimed his gun at him.

The intruder being Beckett Marsh. "Stand down, Renard."

Did Blair call Beckett? It hadn't been quite five minutes. And not enough time for Marsh to have gotten here. So how did he know? "I don't think I will." Beckett's being a SEAL or not, Holt needed an explanation.

"I'm going to put my gun down, then you do the same. Agreed?" Beckett kept his eyes trained on Holt—he was calculating Holt's moves.

But Holt was doing the same.

"Jace called me after Blair left. Said she was worried and she had him concerned, too. I said I'd drive out here on my way into town."

Holt weighed his options. "And if I call Jace right now, he'll confirm what you've said?"

Beckett smirked. "Gigi, come out of the closet."

"Don't move, G," Holt countered. "Call Jace. Put him on speaker. Then I'll let her come out of the closet."

Beckett inhaled. Exhaled. He showed Holt his hands and slowly moved them to his front shirt pocket, retrieving his phone. He dialed. Jace came on speaker. "Beck, you at Hunter's? He and Gigi okay?"

"I'm here. There's been a break-in, but don't come runnin' yet."

"Anyone hurt?"

"I just got here. I'll call you back." He hung up and nodded at Holt. "Confirmation enough?"

"Gigi, come out." Holt shoved his gun in the back of his jeans. "Go outside. Tell Blair you're okay and don't come back in the house. I'll come for you. Understand?"

Gigi stood frozen.

"Gigi, do what Holt says. Go on."

"Where's Hunter?" she asked.

"Go on." Beckett led her from the bedroom and stood in the hall. After a moment, he turned. "You want to tell me what branch of service you work for?"

"DEA." Holt sighed. "I was going to tell you. Eventually."

"I had a hunch from that standoff at her barn. No man in his right mind would have pulled that stunt and gotten in my face. Not in this town."

And why was that?

Beckett nodded toward the front door. "Does she know?"

"No. And you can't tell her."

Beckett grinned. "She's gonna be fit to be tied when she finds out."

Holt stretched out his hand. She was going to be more than that. She was going to hate Holt. "Holt McKnight."

Beckett shook his hand. "You can fill me in on why you're here. After we find Hunter."

Holt followed Beckett into the living room. "Gigi said he went to take the trash out and never came back inside."

"Then let's go check the trash, shall we?" Beckett led the way down the stairs. Blair had Gigi in an embrace. "Hunter? Did you find him?"

Holt ignored her as he and Beckett approached the trash area behind the garage. A black Converse poked out from behind a row of trash barrels.

A pit grew in Holt's stomach. He edged around the dump site.

Hunter lay in a pool of blood.

TEN

Blair sat on the edge of her recliner, staring at a sleeping Hunter and chewing her already nubby thumbnail. Dark hair draped over his bandaged head. He'd taken a couple of stitches to go with his mild concussion and bruised ribs, but Doc Drummond released him to rest at Blair's so Gigi could tend to him. He said he'd come by later and check on him. Little Rocky Balboa had fought hard to protect Gigi.

Gigi brought a tray of tea into the living room, placed it on the coffee table, then took her place beside Hunter. A tear leaked out. "Whoever hurt him could have done way worse. He could have killed him," Gigi murmured.

He could have. And yet, he didn't.

"Do you think it's because I told him everything? Is it my fault?" Gigi asked, eyes wide and filled with guilt.

Blair reached across the coffee table and squeezed her hand. "No way. It's *my* fault. All of it."

"It's nobody's fault," Beckett said, turning his nose up at the tea. Blair had been shocked to see him roll up to Jace's. Guess she'd done a poor job of acting calm at the diner, and Jace had picked up on it, then called Beckett—who had followed them to Doc Drummond's. She couldn't play this off as teenage pranks anymore and Holt had changed his tune, suggesting she come clean with the deputy chief. He'd already probed around on his own anyway and knew most of it. She'd gone into the doc's private office and spilled everything. Even about Mateo. And Hector.

Beckett hadn't batted an eye. Simply told her that everyone makes mistakes and thanked her for finally making his job easier. He also promised to keep her past to himself.

"Any coffee?" Beckett asked. "I don't drink tea."

Holt poured a steaming cup. "I'm a big fan of chamomile."

Blair eyed him and hid a smirk. "Since when?"

"Since the other day." He winked and sipped, his face puckering as if he'd sucked a lemon.

"Yes, I can see how much you love it." She shook her head and said nothing when he placed it back on the tray.

Beckett watched Hunter sleep. "When he wakes up again and feels like it, maybe he'll be able to identify his attacker."

This didn't make sense. Gigi had been tied up but not killed. The house had been trashed. Why would they think Hunter might have something they wanted? She rolled the past events through her mind as she drank her tea and half listened to the conversation going on around her.

I even talked Hunter into a few purchases.

Blair's adrenaline kicked into high gear, but she remained calm. "Gigi, come upstairs with me, will you?" Gigi followed her into Blair's bedroom.

"What's going on?" Gigi glanced behind her and shut the door.

"What did you sell Hunter? You said you talked him into making a purchase. What was it?" She might be grasping at straws, but all these events had happened after that storage auction. She'd placed several things out for sale. What if Hunter bought one or more of those items?

"A hunting knife, a compass…a wooden duck." She shrugged. "Nothing worth hurting us over."

Blair rushed to her laptop on the bed and pulled up the inventory log, scrolling through the items from the storage unit. There. Wooden ducks. Twelve. She'd put one out on the shelf to see how it'd sell before taking up shelf space with the other eleven.

"What are you doing?" Gigi hovered over her shoulder.

She slapped her laptop shut. "You're right. Nothing of value in those items." At least at first glance, but Blair needed to check those ducks, and she wasn't clueing Gigi in. No one else was going to get hurt because of her. "You hungry?"

Gigi ran her hands through her hair. "I could eat. But I'd rather have some answers."

"Me, too, but in the meantime, we have a houseful of people. I'm going to run and grab some pizza or something. Call if Hunter wakes."

Gigi blocked the bedroom door. "You promised me you'd keep me in the loop."

"I did." But this was for Gigi's own good. The only life Blair was willing to risk was her own.

"Hunter could have died, Blair. As in *D-E-A-D*. Dead. Don't keep things from me!" She grabbed Blair's shoulders. "I was strapped to a chair!" She raised her hands, rope burns and bruises revealing her pain. "This isn't going to go away. We have to do something. Drastic."

What exactly did that mean? "Beckett is in the loop now. He has access to things we don't. He can get warrants. Right now he's looking into the Magnolia Inn and a few hotels outside town to see if anyone fitting the description of the man who threatened me might be staying there. And he's going to help look into Jeremy's disappearance."

"Don't lie to me."

"I won't." She swallowed down the guilt.

Gigi waited a beat…two… "Fine. I want extra mushrooms. And Sprite."

"Done." Blair hurried down the stairs and prepared to put on an award-winning performance for Holt. And boom, there he was. "I'm going to get pizza. It's been a long day."

"I'll go with you." Holt grabbed his keys off the coffee table.

Blair groaned inwardly. "I'm capable of going into town and picking up lunch."

Holt swirled his keys around his index finger. "Someone dangerous is running around town. Probably keeping tabs on you. You're not going anywhere alone."

Great. How was she going to get out of this? "Fine. Whatever."

Amused, Holt opened the front door. "Fine. Whatever," he mimicked. Even being stubborn he melted her insides like warm caramel. He opened the truck door for her and she climbed inside.

As they neared the square, Blair glued on her best smile and hoped it worked on him. "I need to grab the receipts from yesterday. Mind dropping me off while you run by Mangiare and pick up the pizzas?"

"Yes." Holt didn't even look her way.

She fluffed her hair, moistened her lips and leaned forward to catch his eye. "Yes, you mind, or yes, you will?"

He came to a halt at the stop sign. His gaze traveled to her lips. "Yes, I mind."

He wasn't budging. Had she lost her touch? Not that she ever really had a touch per se, but… "Come on, Flawless. It'll save us time." She added a little syrup to her smile.

Holt raised an eyebrow. "I'm all for the flirtin', honey. And you look good doin' it, but it ain't your style, so what's really going on?"

Crud. Good looks and a quick mind. Time to think fast. "I need more than five minutes to myself. In my store. With my Christmas trees and lights. And I do need to get some receipts."

Holt heaved a sigh, parked in front of the store. "Why didn't you say that to begin with?"

Because she just now thought it up. "Don't forget G's Sprite."

"I'm going to at least check it out and make sure it's all clear. Then I'll remember the Sprite." He jumped out, went ahead of her and made sure no one was hiding out inside.

"Lock the doors behind you," he said. "I'll be gone six, maybe seven minutes. You said you only needed more than five." He gave her the I'm-serious face.

"Seven, tops." Nerves bunching, she locked the door behind him and left off the lights. She knew exactly where she'd placed the wooden ducks.

She hurried to the back room, kicked a few tubs out of the way and made a beeline for the old box with throw pillows on top. She moved them and grabbed a wooden duck from underneath. Flipping it over, she noticed a small groove. Grabbing a screwdriver off a metal storage shelf, she pried open the bottom.

The air whooshed from her lungs.

This was bad. Really bad. She pulled out another duck, pried it open.

Eleven ducks.

Eleven kilos of cocaine. Worth a fortune for sure.

She sank to her knees. What now? She didn't even know who to contact to give it back. Her heart slammed against her ribs until it hurt. She clutched her chest. Didn't matter that she didn't know who to give them to, she couldn't anyway. These drugs were her only leverage. The only thing that would keep her and Gigi alive—might be the only thing that had been keeping them alive. The minute the cartel members found the cocaine, or she turned it over, they'd kill her for knowing. Might kill everyone close to her to be sure.

Either way, she'd lived long enough in the drug world to know how it worked. The man with the pinky ring would be back. He was already looking in the store. Warning her. Reminding her.

She had to find a new hiding place for the drugs. The cartel was searching for the ducks and it was the only way to throw them off. Scrambling, she opened the remaining ducks, removed the cocaine, then sealed them back up, returning them to the storage bin.

Where wouldn't they think to look if they made another attempt to ransack her store? *Oh, God, please don't let them come back. Help me.*

An idea formed, but she was racing against the clock. Holt would be back in less than five minutes. "God, I hope this is the right decision." Blair couldn't risk telling a single person. Gigi wouldn't be tied to a chair—she'd be dead. And Holt might meet a similar fate to the guy at the bottom of the lake. People just didn't end up that way. He had to be linked to the drugs somehow. And Jeremy. *Oh, God, please!*

She finished hiding the last kilo as Holt's truck pulled up in front of the store. She snatched the tub full of ducks and pillows and met him outside. Holt took the items from her and placed them in the truck bed. "Whatcha got here?"

"Duck decoys and some pillows."

"Gonna cop a comfortable squat while doing a little duck hunting…out of season?"

"Ha-ha. Pizza smells good." She diverted his attention. "Did you get one with extra cheese?"

"Just for you." He winked and opened her door. She hopped in and buckled up. "Do you think Beckett has any new leads about the man who was in my shop? I mean, even if he does, he can't arrest him for buying a cigar box. So then what?"

Holt grimaced. "He...he did find out who he is."

He had? "When? That was fast." Blair opened the pizza box and stole a slice. Holt shot a surprised look her way. "I'm hungry. Sue me."

"He entered the description you gave, including that pinky ring, and it popped. Does the name Alejandro Gonzalez mean anything to you?"

Blair stopped midbite. "Gonzalez?"

Holt glanced over. "Yeah."

The few little bites she'd swallowed stuck in her throat. "I've never seen him...but the name. I've heard the name often. Usually in connection with the Juarez Cartel. Hector said they were responsible for Mateo's death."

"Alejandro?"

Blair nodded. "And another name... Seems like it wasn't a first name but a descriptive name. I can't remember."

Holt gripped the wheel tighter. "That might be pertinent information. Maybe try relaxing—if you can—and it'll come to you."

"Relaxing. Yeah. Piece of cake."

"What did Hector say about Mateo's death?"

"Does it matter?"

"Yes." He turned onto her road. "It does. It could help us—help Beckett."

Blair had worked to push all those memories away and move on. Even put Mateo's cigar boxes out at her store as a way to sell off the memories. She wasn't unaware of the irony. Desiring to give others a fresh start with discarded memories. Adding her own to the mix.

"Hector didn't say much. He came to our house. Told me that Mateo died. He'd been shot. They weren't shipping his body to the States and he'd be buried in Colombia. All I needed to know was that his killer was a family enemy and Hector planned to avenge his brother's death. But I overheard him on the phone and Alejandro was mentioned and then that other name." She racked her brain, but it wouldn't come. *La* was about all she could muster. And the Spanish word for *the* wasn't good enough.

"Did he say which one actually pulled the trigger?"

"It doesn't matter. He'll murder them all." She dropped her half-eaten slice of pizza back in the box. "You don't understand this kind of world, and I wish I didn't. But they're ruthless. Even more so than you see on TV or read about in the news. If the Juarez Cartel is responsible for these attacks, it might be best if you get out of town and take Gigi with you."

"And leave you?" He swerved to the side of the road and slammed on his brakes. "Have you lost your ever-lovin' mind? I'm not going anywhere."

The conviction and loyalty in his voice brought tears to her eyes. "But you could get hurt—again. You don't deserve any of this. Gigi doesn't. No one does. I shouldn't have let you help us so many times. I shouldn't have..." She hung her head. Without meaning to, Blair had come to rely on Holt. And that wasn't fair. If he died, she'd never forgive herself. Now that she knew who was after her, the probability of him losing his life had increased immensely.

He leaned over and cupped her face. "Shouldn't have what?"

"Leaned on you so much."

"I don't mind being your wall, Blair. I kind of rather like it."

Until he ended up dead.

He skimmed his thumb along her cheek, then shifted back into Drive and headed to Blair's. "Do you think Hector knows what's going on?"

"No. He'd have called or paid me a visit. He's lethal, but he's loyal to who he considers family. I suppose on some level that should make me feel comforted, but it doesn't at all."

Holt worked his jaw. "What if he does know?"

"Let's hope he doesn't. He'll come to finish what he started, and I don't want a drug war in my town."

Holt parked behind Beckett's police Bronco and cut the engine. "You sure he still considers you family? What if he knows and is letting this happen to you? Or if he's behind it?"

Blair fitted the cardboard sides back into the pizza box. "I get phone calls every so often. I have to answer. I'm afraid not to."

"What are these phone calls for?" Holt shifted and took the boxes from her.

"Do I need money? Do I need a car? Do I need anything for the business? How's small-town life? Anything new happening? Chitchat." She shrugged. "I always turn him down for the gifts and money and he always ends with 'I am still seeking justice for *our* Mateo.'" A tear slipped down her cheek. "He was never my Mateo. I don't know who he was. It was a game, I guess, to him. Hector says it was to protect me." She laughed but felt no humor. Then she looked at Holt. An amazing, honest man who made her laugh and feel secure. She said Mateo never played pretend, but he'd played the best game she'd ever seen. "He brought me into a dangerous world. A world I promised I'd never be part of again, and here I am. I hate drugs. Everything about them. I don't want this."

Holt leaned over the stack of pizza boxes and hugged her, brushed a kiss to the top of her head. "We'll figure this out. You'll be safe again. I'll do everything I can to make that happen."

"Even work with Beckett. I noticed you two getting along." She broke the embrace and grabbed the Sprite and garlic knots.

"Taking Mitch Rydell's advice and not making enemies."

Blair closed the truck door. Gigi stepped out on the porch. "Hunter's awake and feels like eating. And talking."

A week had passed since Hunter and Gigi were attacked. Now Holt sat in Beckett's cramped office on a sticky Saturday morning drinking a cup of coffee. Beckett had some information and Holt needed a lifeline. Hunter couldn't identify his attacker because of the ski mask. The first blow had been to the back of the head while he was taking out the trash. But Hunter had gotten a punch in before the guy made sure he stayed down.

Hunter had spent Thursday night on Blair's couch. Holt had taken the love seat and Jace had slept in the overstuffed chair. It had been almost comical. Beckett had been the only one to leave.

Blair had acted weird all through dinner, barely touching the pizza she just had to have with extra cheese. She'd claimed she needed some time alone in her shop. At first, Holt had bought the line, but after she'd come out worse than she'd gone in, he'd been convinced something was up.

He'd suspected all along that somehow that storage unit held something the Juarez Cartel wanted. Drugs. Money. Both. Had Blair discovered what it was? Found it? If so, why not confide in him? He'd proven his loyalty. Several times Holt had thought about waking her up and flat-out asking her, but he'd hesitated.

Lines between pretend and reality had blurred dramatically. He'd tried to distance himself, but it didn't work. How was he going to leave this place when his case was closed? Blair might make it easy for him when she found out Jeremy's disappearance was Holt's fault. Right now any ember of hope that had flamed had been doused with lake water. Bryan was dead. Jeremy probably was, too.

No hope. No way for it to rise to the surface.

But he had to wonder, why wasn't the Juarez Cartel coming in and taking care of business as swiftly as was their custom? Not that he was complaining. He wanted Blair and Gigi alive. As he replayed the attacks—other than the snake—it seemed they wanted to scare Blair and Gigi more than kill them. Could be because they wanted the drugs first or it could be because they feared Hector. He already had a score to settle; murdering his sister-in-law would only make things worse.

Keeping things on the down-low kept Hector from getting wind of their attacks and the drugs. If the face behind the Juarez Cartel lived in this small town, he wouldn't want to draw attention to himself. Another drug lord showing up and inciting war would ruin the sweet little life of obscurity he had going here.

"Any news on Alejandro Gonzalez?" Holt asked. "You did call."

Beckett nodded. "I did my own search and called in a few favors. An old SEAL buddy, who would never go into Mexico because that would be illegal, didn't tell me that about six months ago a couple of DEA agents turned up dead in Mexico—I mean Texas—"

"I get it. It's all under the radar. Skip it, I'm not going to say a word. As I've never even been to Mexico to investigate drugs. Or Colombia."

Catching his drift, Beckett nodded and smirked. "The Juarez Cartel intercepted about six million dollars' worth of Hector's powder outside Atlanta a few months ago. Gonzalez's oldest son, Juan, was executed on a yacht in Buenos Aires. My buddy's friend—who's on the inside—said Hector had one of Juan's fingers delivered to Alejandro's home. One finger every week for ten weeks. How's that for vengeance?"

Holt had seen this kind of thing on several occasions.

"Rumor has it Alejandro sent his younger son, Joseph, into the US to hide him from Hector."

Holt chewed on the information. "That's why Alejandro was here. He was visiting his son Joseph." And it explained why the Juarez Cartel continued to threaten Blair and not actually kill her or Gigi. Holt's suspicions had been right. The last place Alejandro would want Hector Salvador was within striking distance of Joseph. Didn't mean they wouldn't attempt to kill Blair if they had to, but they might be trying to work around it, to keep the DEA out of town, to keep any law enforcement from investigating and discovering who headed up the Juarez Cartel.

Which meant if they were willing to keep Blair alive— for now—they might also be keeping Jeremy alive.

But they'd exhausted their little means to search for what they were after. And they hadn't found it. Which meant they would be forced to use drastic measures. Blair was in more danger than ever before.

"You thinking what I'm thinking?" Beckett asked.

"Depends. What are you thinking?"

Beckett raised his eyebrows. "Alejandro may be here to threaten Blair but also move his son so they can take Blair out. If it draws Hector Salvador, Joseph won't be around to become collateral damage or the object of revenge from Mateo's death and the stolen cocaine from Atlanta."

Holt and Beckett were on the same page. "We need to check manifests for private air strips and planes. See if their names are on it. No way they'd go commercial, but it wouldn't hurt to check flights leaving Memphis in the next few days. You have a photo of Joseph? Age?"

"Twenty-four." Beckett grabbed a folder. "No photos. Alejandro guarded his sons fiercely. Especially Joseph.

He was his father's favorite. Never came to the ranch in Mexico, according to my buddy on the inside."

"How very biblical." Holt massaged his tense neck muscles. "Anyone new pop into town in the last few months? Latino?"

"If someone has, I wouldn't necessarily know it. He'd be keeping a low profile."

"Who are your wealthiest citizens? One of them is the face behind the Juarez Cartel. No way this guy would live as a pauper. I've already been keeping my eye out, but no one fits my profile."

Beckett shifted in his chair. "Richest man in town is Mitch Rydell and he uses lots of Latino labor. But Mitch isn't the head of a Mexican cartel. I grew up with him."

Mitch had been on Blair's property that night. "Doesn't mean he's not in cahoots. People change, Beckett. You left for the navy at nineteen. You've only been back in town less than a year. A lot can happen. For many reasons."

"You did do some research on me." Beckett rose and trudged to the window that gave a direct view to the parking lot. "I guess I can ride out there and take a deeper look."

"Want me to go with you?" Holt asked.

"Nah. Don't need Mitch raising questions. I told him I didn't like you." Beckett grinned.

If Holt stayed in Hope, he and Beckett might end up buds. "No harm, no foul. I told Blair the same thing about you."

"Well, now that that's settled…" He chuckled.

Holt wondered if Beckett planned on staying in Hope, as well. A guy with his creds working in this small town didn't make much sense. No action. "How's the sheriff?"

"He won't be able to come back to work. But it could have been worse. Lou's a great guy. I ate Sunday dinner over there often growing up. Miss Ida makes the best fried chicken you ever put in your mouth."

"I love Southern fried chicken." Holt leaned forward, arms across the edge of Beckett's desk. "Why *did* you come back? Heard the rumors about the Secret Service."

Beckett rubbed his forehead. "It's not a rumor. I've turned them down twice now." He laughed, but the sound came across dry and maybe a tad sorrowful. "I like it here."

"So you'll run for sheriff?" What would being the sheriff of a small town be like? Peaceful. Well…considering what was happening now, it wasn't so peaceful, but mostly it was. Be home every night, still be able to keep people safe. The only drugs might be marijuana. Which wasn't small potatoes. Drugs were horrible no matter what kind, and Blair said she wouldn't have any part in that lifestyle again. Didn't matter that Holt was on the right side, he was immersed in the drug world.

"I don't know. I've been offered a job in Atlanta. But there's too many factors to weigh on the side of yes." He waved off the personal information, ending it. "I guess I better get to steppin' if we're going to try to track down Joseph and Alejandro Gonzalez."

Holt finished his coffee and dropped the cup in the trash next to Beckett's desk. "I need to open up the store."

"You say it as if you actually own it."

Part of him wished he did. "It's my cover. If we haven't solved this thing by the Fourth, I will open."

"And Blair?"

"You know the job. The complications that come with it." It had never bothered Holt before. Not until Blair. "If Jeremy's dead…"

"You did everything you could to save him. She'll understand that if you decide to tell her the truth."

"With her history? Drugs are drugs. I don't see any hope for a future."

"But you want it. Which is hope. What you're saying is you have no faith. No anchor to that hope." Beckett stretched. "I know what that's like, Holt. To lose faith. To stopping reaching for hope. It's a miserable way to live."

It was a lonely way to live. Sounded like Beckett might be in the same boat without an anchor. But the pain of losing everything he wanted hurt too much. It was easier to give up. To not expect good things. Then, when faced with utter disappointment and despair, he'd have already been prepared.

And yet had that really taken away the disappointment? The despair? Did not hoping ease the pain when the crushing blow connected with his heart?

No.

Expecting the worst and not allowing his heart to feel didn't bring an iota of peace.

"If she did forgive me I'm not sure how we'd make it work anyway. This is what I do. I'm drowning in everything she hates. No point pursuing it."

Beckett shrugged. "Better to have loved and lost than never love at all. I think. I don't know. Maybe I saw that on a social media post."

Sounded like Beckett got a little too personal again and was backpedaling. Had he come home to nurse his wounds?

What would happen if Holt left when this was over? Without pursuing Blair further?

God, I...I could use some help with the shoveling, if I'm going to dig up some faith. Some hope.

"If I hear anything else, I'll call you." Walking down memory lane must have thrown Beckett for a loop. Pain pulsed behind his dark eyes.

Holt let himself out and ambled down Main Street,

crossing at Read It and Steep. Inside, the little blonde who owned the place stood behind the counter. He couldn't remember her name. Book Lady was all that came to mind, and the fact that she looked way too young to own her own business.

He waved at the uppity lawyer lady who'd been in Beckett's office hunting for information on Bryan Livingston. Beckett said she'd stopped asking when he told her Bryan was a DEA agent and to keep that confidential.

She gave him a half wave and moved along toward the courthouse. Only woman in town who didn't make with the niceties and chitchat. Folks passed that aloofness off as her being snooty. Holt had suspicions she was hiding something. But that wasn't any of his...

That was when he saw it.

Painted across his window in hunter green. The Great Outdoors. Pine trees had been painted at the corners of the words. It hit his gut with force. This store was real. But it wasn't his.

How had...? He stepped up to the shiny window, his reflection staring back at him—the liar. The man Blair wouldn't want to be with when she discovered the truth.

The man who might not want to only pretend this was his place and his life anymore.

A ray of light peeked through the casket of his heart and shone a ray on the decayed hope there.

"What do you think?" Blair's voice floated on the early morning breeze before her reflection came into view.

"When did you do this?" He pivoted and gaped. Hair swept up all messy-like in a knot on her neck. A soft red dress that stopped in time for him to admire her lovely calves.

"I called Mr. Weston last week when you nailed down the store name. Looks good, huh?"

Better than. He unlocked the door. "You amaze me, Blair. You think of everything."

"It's the least I could do after everything you've done for me. I didn't…I didn't trust you in the beginning. Trust is really hard for me after Mateo. But I do now, and I know you'd never lie or deceive me. You're not him. You're nothing like him."

No amount of light was going to resurrect dead hope. Not with words like this that touched places he'd long buried. He swallowed and kneaded his neck muscles, unsure of what to do. If he wasn't lying and deceiving he'd have swept her up in a kiss made for the movies.

But he was. And he was utterly sick over it.

"Thank you, Blair. For the window…and for your faith in me." Even if he was lying because of his job, he could be trusted to protect her and do the right thing by Jeremy and this case.

She pointed to the sign. "It's time to make your window display."

Good. A change of topic. He was having trouble reining in his emotions right now. "No Christmas lights."

"A few Christmas lights." She smirked and slipped inside the store. "We need stars. I'm thinking all about under the moonlight."

He followed her into the back room and studied her as she pilfered around. She snagged a navy blue pup tent. "Let's pop it."

An hour later, Holt stood in astonishment at the scene Blair had brought to life. A tent stood in the corner. She'd used logs, ash and battery-operated candles to produce a campfire. White lights hung like twinkling stars and she'd used three different-sized Christmas trees to create a forest.

She beamed and clasped her hands. "I've grown to like having you next door."

He'd grown to like being next door.

"I need to get my shop opened. Mrs. McKay said the inn was full and a group was heading out to the bike trails, but some of the women were shopping this morning."

Holt ambled along beside her. She opened her shop door and froze.

"What's the matter?" He scanned the store. Listened.

"Someone's been in here." She walked to the register, bent over to pick up a few ink pens on the floor, then placed them in the holder. "These were in the holder last night. And it feels weird. Like…like a presence is here." She whipped her head toward the window display and gawked.

"What aren't you telling me?" She'd been keeping her motives about stopping by here since last week a secret. What did she know?

The back door slammed.

Holt's pulse soared, and he zipped through the store toward the back exit.

Blair clutched her throat and prayed for Holt. Chasing criminals wasn't smart.

It was only a matter of time before they'd come back. Blair had kept her discovery bottled up since Thursday, afraid that confiding might be worse than keeping it quiet. She was lying to guard Gigi and Holt. But was that the right thing to do? To withhold information? Blair wasn't sure. Holt had been nothing but honest with her.

About his past.

About losing his faith. But anything that was lost could be found. Blair was living proof. Right now all she had was faith that God would keep her, Holt and Gigi safe.

And Jeremy.

What if Jeremy wasn't safe, though? Could she handle it? Did that mean God couldn't be trusted?

She rushed to the front of the store, jumping the picket fence that was part of the window display, and scanned the area outside. No one watching. She'd hidden the cocaine in the wrapped Christmas boxes under the Christmas tree. One kilo in each box. Hiding in plain sight. Lifting each box lid, she let out a pent-up breath. Not that having cocaine in her possession gave her any relief. But that meant whoever had been in here didn't have it. And she had more time. Time to…what? Make a trade for Jeremy? No, they'd kill them both. She wouldn't call Hector. Her only choice was to call the DEA and risk the whole town knowing her past.

She closed the lids and bent over, breathing deep.

"Blair!" Holt hollered as he rushed inside. "He got away. None of this started until you purchased that storage unit. There's got to be drugs or money or both inside. Somewhere. They've searched everything and everywhere. If you know something…"

Blair couldn't peer into his eyes and lie. Could she? Stomach churning, heart palpitating near the point of cardiac arrest, she pressed her lips together. Telling him put him at risk. Not telling him kept him at risk. Which was the safer choice?

Did she trust this man? Yes.

Did she love him? Yes. *Oh boy.*

When you loved someone, you were honest. "I'm going to tell you something. Because I believe in being honest with the person you…you care about. No secrets. I found what they wanted. I'll tell you what it is but I'm not telling you what I did with it. It'll keep you safer if you don't know."

Holt's eyes held that same tortured expression she'd seen on a few occasions, as if he didn't want her to confide in him—even if he did ask for it. She couldn't quite make out what to think about that.

"What did you find, Blair?"

She stepped closer, grabbed his hand.

"What did you find?" he murmured.

"Eleven kilos of what I think is cocaine. I found them in the big wooden ducks. Hunter bought one that night his place was tossed. If we ask him about it—which we won't—I'm guessing he'll say it's missing. So there's twelve kilos if you count that one."

Holt raked a hand through his hair. "Who knew Hunter bought the duck? Other than Gigi. Someone had to have seen him buy it. We need to ask Gigi who else was in the store at that time."

"Let's hope she remembers."

ELEVEN

Blair sat on the banks of her pond, the scent of earth and fish invading her senses. The sun edged under the horizon, leaving it in swaths of orange, violet, fuchsia and periwinkle. Holt hadn't left her store all afternoon. Not with the steady stream of tourists from the Magnolia Inn. Every time the bell had rung, her stomach lurched for fear it would be Alejandro Gonzalez again.

Twice Holt had asked if she'd share where she'd hidden the cocaine.

Twice she told him he was better off not knowing. It didn't seem to matter how many times she explained Hector's ruthlessness or capability to maim and murder, Holt wouldn't give up or run away. She admired his bravery, loyalty and strength, but she feared something terrible might happen to him. Instead, he ground his jaw and kept that cool look in his eyes. Yeah, he was mad. But she'd rather him be mad than dead.

A bull frog croaked as a fish plopped in and out of the water, leaving soft ripples in its wake. Just as Blair's past romantic choice had left a string of ripples, stretching into the here and now. Threatening everyone she loved.

With choices came consequences, and she'd accepted that. God had been gracious to her. But what was happening now hadn't been a consequence, had it? She'd bought one lousy storage unit. Anyone could have bought the thing and they'd be in Blair's shoes now. Ronnie's broken-down truck had been a blessing in disguise for him. He had a wife and two kids. These heinous criminals wouldn't hesitate to use children as leverage—or to take one of their lives. The drugs they trafficked erased the lives of children every day.

She could use a blessing right now. She stood and dusted her damp hands on her jeans as she headed to the house. Better to be inside come dark-thirty. She edged the tree line.

A twig snapped.

An eerie chill finger-walked up her back.

She needed to move forward, but fear kept her planted to the ground, scanning the thick cluster of trees. She swallowed and forced a step…then another.

Continued crunching of leaves and snapping of twigs matched the blood whooshing in her ears. She broke into a sprint when, suddenly, a biting pain ripped through her skull. Someone had yanked a handful of her hair.

She cried out and worked to wiggle free, but her attacker had an iron grip. "Where is it, Blair? What have you done with it?"

The voice sounded distorted, but familiar. Where had she heard it before? "I don't know what you're talking about! I don't have anything." He had her in a choke hold, forcing her breaths to come in gasps.

"You leave it in your back room—unlocked—by midnight. Or everyone dies!"

She landed an elbow to his sternum and he grunted. She broke free and raced across her yard toward Holt's house, praying he was still there.

She smacked straight into him in her driveway.

"Whoa, honey!" Realization dawned in his eyes and

he blinked, then darted a glance to the woods. "Where?" Already he was racing toward them.

"The east side!" she hollered. "Holt!"

"Get in the house!"

She flew up the porch and into the living room. Gun. She needed her gun. Hurrying to the kitchen, she snatched it up and headed for the back door. Holt couldn't be out there alone.

The knock on the front door sent her two feet in the air. Holt peeped in the window. Blair hurried and unlocked it.

"Same truck I saw the other day just blew down the street. He'd be long gone by the time I pulled out of here. Did he hurt you? Say anything?" Holt grabbed her face and inspected her. Then he brought her close and kissed her forehead. "Why were you outside?"

"I guess part of me wants to believe I'm still secure on my own property." She relished his strength, his warmth.

"What happened?"

She relayed the events. Even what the attacker said.

Holt led her to the couch and put his arm around her. "Well, that's out of the question. You can't give them the drugs."

"I know," Blair whispered. "I think I need to tell Beckett. Or the DEA or something. But if they get wind, they'll kill Gigi. Kill you."

Holt fidgeted while he stared at the ceiling, as if battling a mammoth decision. Well, they did have a mammoth decision to make. "I'm going to do one more check. You'll be all right?"

"Yeah." She locked the door after he left, put on a kettle of tea and waited until the whistle blew, startling her. She poured a cup of chamomile tea to try to soothe her frayed nerves.

Holt knocked lightly on the front door. Had to be Holt. *God, please let it be Holt.*

It was.

Blair let him inside. "Anything?" His jaw was clenched and his nostrils flared. Something had royally ticked him off. "Nothing." He scowled and pinched the bridge of his nose.

A beat of silence passed.

"Did you talk to Hunter?"

Holt collapsed on the couch. "He said no one had been inside the shop that he remembered, but he talked to several people after he left. Anyone could have seen him with the duck, because it wasn't in a bag. But no one specifically asked about it."

Something really had Holt irritated.

"Did he give you any names? Of the people he talked to?"

Holt grimaced. "Mitch Rydell. The old lady from the Magnolia Inn, the tea lady, the Daniels lady, Ronnie Lawson, Jace…to name a few. The guy who owns that old music store and the woman who runs the candle shop. Hunter Black is right chatty."

"So basically the whole town." Blair sank next to him. "You give him the description of the man in my shop?"

"Yes." Holt sat next to her, slipped his arm back around her shoulder and rubbed her upper arm, but his touch felt tense.

"I'm afraid. I'm afraid for us all. And for Jeremy. Could he be in cahoots with this man?"

Holt blew out a breath. "It's possible Jeremy might have latched on to some information at his work about drug trafficking. And he may have gotten caught."

"Did Beckett find that out?" Had Jeremy tried to do the right thing, only to be hurt?

Holt squeezed her shoulder. "Beckett's working hard. So is my private investigator. It seems like the storage unit might have been a drop-off site for the traffickers."

Blair shook her head. "But why dump drugs in a storage container that anyone could buy?"

Holt leaned his elbows on his knees. "Either they ended up in that container by mistake or they accidentally auctioned off the wrong container."

Blair rubbed Holt's back. "You regret getting out of your truck that day?" She tried to half laugh, to make light of it, but the truth was she'd brought Holt into a dark world.

He sat up and the intensity in his eyes sent a warm tingle through her. He framed her face. "I don't regret any of this. I certainly don't regret you. I don't regret our kiss—"

"Kisses," she countered, her heart thrumming.

Leaning in, he whispered, "Kisses." His lips touched hers like an airy feather.

Glass shattered the front window, and stuffing sprayed from the couch.

Blair screamed.

Holt flipped her to the floor at lightning speed and shielded her with his body.

Another shot fired and the vase on the end table next to the couch exploded. Holt flipped the coffee table over and used it to cover them. "We have to get out through the kitchen."

Blair's ears rang; everything sounded as if it were underwater.

Holt's gun glinted under the dim light. "Crawl to the back door. I'm right behind you."

Glass shards on the floor left stings as they pierced her skin, but she continued army crawling.

Crack!

A lamp blew up.

It was almost like their attackers were aiming for glass items.

Holt fired his weapon out the window.

Blair inched toward the kitchen and back door. The smell of gunfire and fear permeated the air.

Picking her up off the floor, Holt swung the door open, hurdled outside and scanned the area. "Head for the pasture." He grabbed her hand and they sprinted across the yard. Summer heat wilted Blair's hair to her already sweaty face. Her lungs burned as her eyes adjusted to the darkness.

Holt switched directions, dragging Blair with him, nearly knocking her off balance.

The sound of metal hitting metal echoed. "They hit the tractor by the barn. We're going through the woods," he bit out.

"But someone was in the woods. What if it's an ambush?" Blair couldn't see a thing, but she believed in Holt and his sense of direction.

He growled, zigzagging north, ducking low as they ran behind a row of baby pine trees on the edge of the property. They were double-backing to the front of the house where the shooter had been.

"You wouldn't happen to have your keys, would you?" he barked.

"No."

She guessed he didn't, either.

Holt cursed under his breath and darted across and down the road toward a neighbor's home, sending Blair into a stumble. "Sorry, honey. We've got to move."

In the neighbor's yard, Holt pointed with his gun. "ATV. Let's go."

"You want to steal their children's four-wheeler?"

Holt skidded to a halt in front of it. "You want to knock on their door and invite them into this mess?"

"No." Blair stared at the red four-wheeler. "I don't see the key. Now what?"

Holt searched the yard. Stopped his gaze on the work

truck in the driveway. He hopped off the four-wheeler and rifled through the bed of the truck, bringing up a screwdriver. "Now we borrow it without asking. Get on!"

Blair gawked. She'd never stolen anything in her life!

"Get on!" he growled.

Blair did exactly what he said and gawked again when Holt ripped the ignition from the top console, exposing the wires as he worked to remove it. He slung the part with the key hold on the ground, then yanked the starter, bringing it roaring to life. Tossing one last glance back at the neighbor's home, he hollered, "Hang on!" over the deafening motor.

Blair clung to his waist for dear life as he peeled out of the yard and barreled down the road. The wind, hot and sticky, blew in her face, causing her hair to flail and sting her cheeks.

Headlights blinded them. Blair spun around to see a truck gaining, but the beams were too bright for her to identify the driver.

She ducked her head, resting her brow on Holt's back. He made a hard right, causing the wheels on the left side to lift off the ground. She clung tighter and held in a wail.

The truck inched closer, lights continuing to blind her.

"Holt!" she screamed.

Swerving off the road, he cut a left and dipped into a ditch, sending them airborne and into a soybean field. Switching gears, Holt bucked and tossed them, but he didn't let up. Dirt and soybean plants exploded into the air and pelted their skin.

The lights disappeared down the road and Holt brought the four-wheeler to a stop, letting it idle. Blair collapsed against his back and breathed deeply. He took her arms, which were still around his waist, and held them tight against him, stroking the side of her hand with his thumb.

"How did you know how to do that?"

"Don't all country boys do that?" He laughed softly and brought her hand to his lips and kissed it, but never turned to look at her.

Why would they give her a drop-off time for their stash and then come right back and try to kill her or kidnap her? Something didn't make sense. Either way she was thankful Holt had showed up. Blair was well aware what came with a cartel kidnapping.

Torture.

Sunday morning, Holt sat across from Beckett at the Black-Eyed Pea and salted his home fries. It was business as usual in Hope. As if there weren't a drug cartel in town. As if Blair hadn't almost been abducted. As if bad things weren't happening to the people he loved.

"Where's she staying?" Beckett asked.

"I told her she couldn't go back home. Especially with the mess the assailants left behind. Mr. Weston reinstalled her windows this morning." Blair hadn't gone to church and opted to clean up her house. "I let her and Gigi stay at my place." He'd taken down the surveillance equipment the day after he started sleeping on her couch. Couldn't get any closer than that.

"The Millers reported their four-wheeler stolen."

"It's in my garage. I'm trying to keep what's happening as hushed as I can. I know how Blair feels about her reputation in this town. She doesn't want people to find out about her past." Holt sipped his coffee.

"They think it was a high school prank. So you're home free. Tonight, you can put it back in the bean field, and I'll haul it to their house. Tell them where I found it and leave it at that." Beckett toyed with a biscuit.

The easy atmosphere did nothing to soothe Holt's taut nerves. Someone had tried to make Blair disappear. Holt guessed they didn't count on him being there. More than likely, they didn't care and had every intention of disposing of him, too.

Holt's phone dinged, alerting him to a text. He checked the screen. "This is interesting. We were looking into a guy named Keith Hill. Worked with Jeremy and had a few drug possession charges. He's missing."

"How long?"

"Hasn't shown up for work since Friday. The manager says he won't answer his calls or return voice mails. Sounds a lot like Jeremy Sullivan's vanishing act."

Beckett tapped his fork on his lower lip. "You think this Keith ran the drugs and money and Jeremy found out, so they abducted or killed Jeremy and then killed Keith, too?"

That was an excellent question. "Could be doing away with collateral damage. Who knows? They're merciless. They might have killed him simply for allowing someone to get information on them. I'm hoping they have Jeremy and are—" he swallowed "—questioning him for information." *Torture* was the right word, but it implied Jeremy wasn't dead...yet.

"I don't get why you would place drugs in a storage container you know is going to be auctioned off?"

"Something fell through the cracks. Auctioned the wrong unit or misplaced the drugs." Unless... Holt excused himself, leaving the building to have some privacy, and called his handler.

"You got my text?" Drake asked.

"Yeah. I was curious about Hollow Chest again. Any new information or connections? The managers, owners, auctioneers...one or all have to be in on this on some level."

"Looking into that now. But we do have something else. I was about to call you. We searched Keith Hill's next of kin and something interesting popped up. His cousin lives in Hope. Owns a used sporting goods store on the outskirts of town."

Holt's stomach bottomed out. "Ronnie Lawson."

"Yeah. Ronnie Lawson."

Ronnie hadn't been at the storage auction that day.

But he was supposed to be. He'd asked to see the storage items. Blair had mentioned she was glad he wasn't there, because he would have outbid her.

Storing drugs in the containers wasn't such a risk if the buyer had an endless supply of cash to outbid everyone else. It would be easy to walk right off the lot with a truckload of drugs or cash. No one would suspect anything shady because the public could come and bid. Genius. Except Ronnie's truck had broken down.

Blair got caught in the crosshairs.

This must be what Jeremy had discovered. But Keith or Ronnie or someone else either caught Jeremy nosing around the storage units or discovered he had knowledge of the operation and kidnapped him. Or killed him.

God, let him be alive.

"Any rap sheet on Ronnie Lawson?" Holt asked.

"No, but I just received the information, so I'll keep searching. Lived in Hope his whole life."

"What about Keith? Can you send over a picture of him?" Maybe Blair would recognize him.

"Grew up in Memphis. It's sent."

They might work for the cartel, but neither man ran it. So who did? "I'm going to pay Ronnie Lawson a visit." Would Ronnie have taken out his own cousin? Or had the cartel? Holt knocked on the window and motioned Beckett outside, then told him what he knew. His phone dinged and he showed Beckett the photo of Keith Hill. Blond hair, blue eyes, horse-sized teeth. "You recognize him?"

Beckett shook his head. "You want me to go over to Lawson's? Shake the tree and hope something falls?"

"No. I think I'll handle this one."

"You're emotionally invested. Keep a cool head, man."

Holt nodded and jogged to his truck. Eight minutes later, he pulled into Ronnie's drive.

Ronnie was nowhere to be found. "Lawson!" Holt entered the kitchen. Eggs still sat on the counter with a tub of butter. Bread remained in the toaster, toasted. Holt drew his weapon and searched the house. Nothing out of place.

At the back door, he froze.

The glass was smeared with blood.

Mr. Weston had repaired the window and Blair sat at her kitchen counter drinking a cup of coffee but not enjoying it. Holt had been with Beckett all morning trying to run down leads. He'd called earlier and told her he would be home for lunch. He'd used the word *home*.

Yeah, Holt's faith was shaky. But he was a believer. And Blair prayed and believed he'd renew that faith. He even admitted he wanted to. Shaky faith was more faith than Mateo had. He never claimed to be a Christian and Blair had been so enamored by his lavish life, his smooth but empty words and promises, and his extravagant gifts that she believed he was everything she ever wanted. They'd have beautiful babies, stay grounded in one place to raise them and she'd have her happily-ever-after.

She couldn't have been more wrong. She wanted nothing to do with that life. When she thought of her future, only one man came to mind. Holt. But in order to have a future with him, they would both have to make it out of this mess alive.

Her thoughts turned to Gigi, yet another loved one in danger. She was at the senior center with Hunter today. Still, Blair felt the need to check in on her and sent her a text. A minute later Gigi replied that she was fine. She'd been acting funny the last couple of days. Blair couldn't blame her, though. A giant target was on her back—thanks to Blair—and Hunter had been injured. They'd been inseparable since. One of the only decent things to come out of her latest run-in with the Juarez Cartel.

Eventually, she was going to have to tell Dad about her former life. About her thoughts on what had happened to Jeremy. But she wanted some concrete answers first. She dumped her cold coffee in the sink and rinsed the cup.

Gravel crunching drew her attention to the living room window. Doc Drummond's silver Mercedes was in the drive. He stepped out and reached inside, brought out a pan covered in foil.

Blair laughed. Looked like they'd be having enchiladas for lunch.

She opened the door and Doc held up the casserole dish. "I guess you know what's in here."

Blair motioned him inside. The scent of beef, tomatoes and green chilies filled her living room. "You didn't have to do this. But Gigi will be over-the-moon. I'll go put it in the kitchen. Tell Sophia and Riella thank you."

"It's hot." He handed her the dish with the oven mitts and followed her into the kitchen. "Thought we'd ignore your declines and bring them anyway. You've been through a lot lately, Blair."

"Well, you're all very thoughtful."

"Where is she? Gigi."

"Sunny Living." Blair turned the oven on warm and slid the enchiladas in. "Why?"

"I was just there checking on a patient. I didn't see her."

That was odd.

She closed the oven door and stood.

Doc Drummond clamped his hand around her mouth from behind. "This won't hurt. Just a little stick."

TWELVE

The smell of hay and horse manure assaulted Blair's nose. She blinked as her vision cleared. Her hands were bound to the back of a wooden chair and her feet were tied to the legs.

Panic shot a jolt of adrenaline through her, snapping her out of her daze as she pulled and writhed to gain freedom.

Doc Drummond had injected her with a sedative of some kind. Why? And she'd been tossed in a stable. But where? Mitch Rydell's?

Were Doc and Mitch working with the cartel? Doc did do some pro bono work in South America. Could he have become entangled while down there? He made plenty of money, he had no reason for dirty cash. Except greed.

Wait… No… Doc owned a set of stables, too.

The hay tickled her nose and she sneezed. Something lay in a heap across from her.

The heap moved. It was a man.

Ronnie Lawson. Ronnie? Oh no! What did he have to do with this?

His hands were tied behind his back and blood trickled down his cheek. "Ronnie," she whispered, trying to tamp down her anxiety. "Wake up."

Ronnie moaned and struggled to get into a sitting position. "Blair?"

"Yes, it's me. Why did Doc Drummond bring you here?"

"I'm so sorry," he rasped. "I didn't mean for this to get so out of hand. I was... I needed the money." Ronnie leaned his head against the wooden stable wall, the hay rustling underneath his long legs.

"What are you talking about? Let what get out of hand?" Her hands trembled behind her as she struggled to try to free herself from the ropes that bound her, ignoring the burn cutting across her wrists.

"You weren't supposed to purchase that unit. I was. But my truck..."

Realization struck her with a thud. "You're a drug runner? You?"

Ronnie avoided eye contact, focusing instead on the stable wall. In the distance horses neighed and pawed at their doors. A dog barked. "My business was going down the tubes. I was in serious financial straits. Dawn was threatening to leave me. I went to see Doc about my blood pressure, told him about my stress, and he offered me a way to climb out. To make some serious cash. All I had to do was find a way to drive to Texas. I brought Keith in."

Blair wrinkled her nose and shook her head. "Who's Keith?"

"My cousin. Works with your brother, Jeremy. Over-the-road driver. Texas run."

Jeremy! Dread punched her ribs. "What happened? What did you do to him? Where is he?"

Ronnie sniffed and hung his head. "It got out of control. Too fast."

Blair's throat closed, but she forced the question again. "Where is my brother?"

"He knew too much. Keith caught him. Jeremy admitted he'd been working for a DEA agent. Jeremy shouldn't have followed Keith to the storage unit."

"What did he do, Ronnie?"

Ronnie's eyes glazed over. "Keith handed off the items filled with drugs to the manager who put them in the unit to be auctioned off. My job was to come in and bid. Make it all look legit. Keep the cops away. Easy. Everyone got their cut."

Even Doc Drummond. Blair's mind reeled. "You were buying units loaded with drugs. Using drug money." No wonder he could always outbid her. "Doc Drummond gave you the money?" He was connected to the Juarez Cartel?

"I'm sorry. I had to make up for my mistakes or they'd kill me. I never wanted to hurt you, Blair. Just scare you."

Blair struggled, but the ropes were too strong. "You ran me off the road?"

"Keith and Manny. They were going to wreck you… and take the ducks with the cocaine. But you fired on them!"

"Manny. Sophia's brother? He's in on this with Doc Drummond, too?" He drove her and Holt back to the lake after they found the dead DEA agent. Blair squeezed her eyes shut. "You tried to shoot me down, abduct me and terrorize me! You put a snake in my bed!"

"That wasn't me. I didn't do that. I wanted to find the drugs and save Keith. Save myself. That's it. I'm not a killer. I was desperate. I wanted to scare you in the woods, get you to make the drop, but by that time it was too late. I'd failed. Manny was sent in to take you in or take you out."

Manny had shot at her, but he hadn't counted on Holt being there and hot-wiring that four-wheeler.

Ronnie wiped his eyes on his knees. "I couldn't save Keith. He made a mistake by killing your brother. He paid for it. And now they're going to kill us, too."

Time stopped. Blood whooshed in Blair's ears. Bile rose in her throat. "My brother's dead?"

"I'm sorry," he whispered. "It…it got way out of hand."

Jeremy had died working for the DEA. "Who was this DEA agent? Do you know? Did he say?"

"No. Wouldn't give him up. He tried to get Keith to flip. But…but it got so out of hand."

"Stop saying that!" His mystery friend had to be the agent. That was why Jeremy wouldn't talk about him. He'd protected him even when it killed him. *Oh, Jeremy.* How did he know a DEA agent? Had he been arrested or mixed up in some kind of bust and the DEA agent took pity on him? Didn't matter now.

This agent had gotten her brother clean.

Then got him killed.

No wonder they couldn't find anything on him. Blair's eyes filled with tears; they ran hot down her cheeks. "The man in the lake. Who was he?"

"I don't know. I suspect he had something to do with the drugs. If I hadn't broken down on the interstate, none of this would have happened."

"If you hadn't chosen to run drugs, none of this would have happened." Blair couldn't handle the excruciating pain. "Where? Where did my brother die? How?"

Ronnie buried his head in his knees and cried.

"Answer me!"

Sounds of hooves approaching caught her attention. They would torture her for the drugs. Doc had to be working for the man who came into the store that day. He might have been staying here at Doc's place. It could be him now.

A man's gravelly voice sounded. Muffled. In Spanish. But Blair knew the language. A younger voice spoke back. They were discussing what to do with Ronnie and saying that Joseph needed to get out of town now more than ever. If Hector found out.

Hector! Did they think Blair would have gone to Hector? Maybe she should have.

No. No she needed to rely on God to get her out of this. To have some mercy on her. Ronnie looked at her. "He died at the storage unit. Keith shot him. He called me and I came. We loaded Jeremy's body into his truck and drove it to my shop."

"Where is he now?"

"We—"

"Hola, Hermosa." The man from the shop opened the stable door, sinister eyes boring into hers. "Do you know who I am?"

Alejandro Gonzalez. "Don't call me beautiful."

He chuckled and stepped into the stables, then glanced at Ronnie and curled his lip. He sat on a feed bucket across from Blair. "I see why Mateo had such interest in you. Feisty." He grabbed her face with one hand and squeezed until she was sure her jaw would break. "I asked you a question. Do you know who I am?"

If she told him the truth, they'd know she'd brought the cops in. They already suspected it. Tears slid down her cheeks. "No."

He released his grip, but the ache continued. "I wasn't so sure at first. The fact that you moved here. Hector's sister-in-law." He rubbed his chin. "We watched you. No contact with Hector." He touched her knee and she flinched. *"Coneja asustada."* He laughed. "No, you're not in on this. It's not in your eyes."

He was right; she was a scared rabbit. "I left that life. I didn't steal your drugs."

"The snake in your bed told the tale. If you were connected to Hector, you'd have called him. Known it was us. Brought him here. You passed that test."

"Test! I could have died. And you'd never have found your drugs."

Alejandro shrugged. "I was willing to take that chance.

But you passed. And here we are. And there is no Hector to save you."

Blair bit the inside of her lip to keep it from trembling. "You're afraid of Hector?"

He laughed. "Alejandro Gonzalez is afraid of no one. I have a score to settle with that pig. But I want my son long gone on a plane first." He stood, walked around Blair and grabbed her index finger, twisting it until blinding pain forced her to cry out. "And tomorrow I'm going to start with this finger and send him one every single week until all your fingers are gone. Like he did with my son."

God, help me! "If you kill me you'll never find the drugs."

He laughed in her ear, the smell of Cuban cigars filling her nostrils.

"By finger number three, you'll tell me," he whispered. He kissed the top of her head, patted her shoulder in a fatherly way and left the stall. Her choice backfired. She'd once again made the wrong decision. But this time, she would pay with her life.

Holt raced to Blair's. Ronnie was in the middle of this and had been broken down on the side of the road when he should have been buying the storage unit.

The fact that he was missing and foul play was at hand didn't sit well. Keith was gone, too. The cartel's key players were removing anyone connected with their plot, which meant they might be uprooting. Somehow Ronnie and Keith had gotten mixed up as grunt men. Alejandro would never have been in town to meet with a low-level runner. He was here to see his son—if his son was indeed in Hope—or he'd been here meeting with the head of the cartel.

Anyone could blend in, including Joseph Gonzalez.

Beckett might not have found anything suspicious at Mitch Rydell's, but that didn't mean there wasn't anything to be found. How did Keith and Ronnie get mixed up in this? Someone had approached them. Bribed them. Or offered an amount of money they couldn't pass up. Holt slowed on Blair's road. A car he'd never seen before was parked in her drive. Sleek black sedan. Memphis plates. A rental?

He eased out of his truck and drew his weapon, inching up the walk but keeping from the windows. The front door stood ajar. Pushing it open with his foot, he entered the living room. Nothing out of place.

He cleared it and moved to the kitchen.

A man with his back to him held a syringe.

"Hands up. Slowly."

The man turned. If Holt didn't already recognize him, he'd think a celebrity had made himself at home. The man had quite a presence.

Hector Salvador.

"You must be Mr. Renard. Although I suspect you're not who you claim to be. Your entry into town and into my sweet Blair's life seems a tad too coincidental." He smirked. "Put the gun down. I mean you no harm. I'm here to protect what's mine."

Heat filled Holt's gut. "Blair doesn't belong to you."

"She's *familia*." He held up the syringe. "And she's been taken."

The blood drained from Holt's face. "By who? What is that?"

"A tranquilizer of some kind. And I think we both know by whom." Hector laid it on the counter.

Holt had a million questions, but they'd have to wait. If Gonzalez had Blair, time was of the essence. He could be torturing her for the cocaine right now. "How did you know she was in trouble?"

"Gigi called me a few days ago. I got here as soon as I could. Apparently, in the nick of time." He showed his straight pearly whites. "I can see you don't like this, no?"

No. No, he didn't. Hector would choose drugs over Blair.

"I feel partly to blame," Hector crooned.

"You cut his son's fingers off one by one and had them sent to him by courier. I'd say you're fully responsible."

"I didn't buy that storage unit." Hector rounded the counter. Holt aimed his gun. Hector didn't even flinch. He knew Holt needed him to find Blair. It sickened Holt, but it was true. "He killed my brother. He stole from me. He deserved it. And I'm far from done with him, even now."

Holt didn't care about the war raging between the cartel leaders, but he didn't want Blair caught in the crosshairs.

"Was the door unlocked when you got here?" Holt asked.

Hector nodded. "*Sí.* Gigi says that Alejandro is here. Of course, she had no idea of his name, but she described him. Have you seen him?"

Holt shoved his gun in his waistband and examined the syringe. "No. We've been searching."

"You have another undercover DEA agent positioned?"

"No." No point hiding what Hector had already picked up on. He didn't evade arrest this long by being stupid. The man was something straight out of a gangster movie. Holt took in Hector's charming smile. The amused gleam in his eyes. His white dress shirt and black dress pants probably cost more than what Holt made in a year. He couldn't trust this guy, but he needed his help because he had a feeling Hector knew where Blair might be. He divulged everything including the fact that Blair had inadvertently stolen the cocaine.

"Where is it? The product?" Hector asked.

"She wouldn't tell me."

Hector laughed. "I've always been impressed with Blair. Smart. Soft."

Holt wanted to punch the smugness off his face. Instead, he balled his fist and clenched his back teeth, gun in hand.

"You don't like me talking about her fondly." Hector laughed. "You are fascinated by her, too."

"No. I'm in love with her."

Hector grunted. "You say Joseph might be hiding here. Alejandro wouldn't put his son's life into just anyone's hands." Stroking his chin, he leaned on the counter. "That must mean one thing."

Holt stared him down. Everything inside him told him this was wrong, fraternizing with the enemy. But Blair's life was at stake. And he'd do whatever he had to in order to save her. "What?"

Hector shook his head and laughed. "Smart. So very smart. La Mujer is here. I thought she'd gone back to Mexico, but—"

"La Mujer?" The woman? "Who is La Mujer?"

"You don't know, Agent?" Hector tsked him. "Of course you don't. You're all pathetic. Running around with guns trying to eradicate all the bad men and their drugs from the earth. Such false hope. You will never be able to rid the world of men like me. Businessmen. We evolve. Find new avenues. Stay steps ahead of you."

Holt burned to end this man. But he was speaking the truth. For every cartel member they put away, a new one arose. For every pipeline they uncovered, ten more emerged as fast as the authorities could throw the book at them.

But they couldn't stop trying.

And that…that was hope. Hope for a better future. For a future in general. "What is it I don't know?"

"The head of the Juarez Cartel isn't a man. She's a woman."

Holt stepped back, stunned. "A woman?"

"She traveled to the States for education many years ago, where I met her. Came back home to Mexico and murdered her half brothers when her father got sick in order to rise to power. She's even more deadly than Gonzalez. I should know." He pointed to his cheek. Underneath the day-old growth, a faint scar ran the length of it. "And that was when we were lovers." He inhaled as if remembering fond but dark memories.

"Why is she here?"

Hector's eyes hardened. "It's not your concern right now. Getting Blair back is."

Hector was withholding information. Holt knew he was lying. Fernando Juarez was dead and his sons had been murdered via coral snakes. "Juarez never had a daughter. Why are you lying?"

Hector wagged a finger at Holt. "I am many things, but I am not a liar. You don't listen. Fernando had a daughter out of wedlock. Not a Juarez. A Menendez. He gave her the *madre*'s surname to protect his baby from rival cartels and other enemies. I said she murdered her *half brothers*."

Menendez. Why did that name sound familiar? Holt sniffed. "Do you smell that?"

Hector frowned. Followed the scent and opened the oven. "Enchiladas."

Enchiladas.

Sophia Menendez. The Drummonds' housekeeper? She'd be around the same age as Hector, or a little younger. It was hard to tell. They both looked very young. But it fit.

No. Way.

"I know where Blair is."

"And so do I, Agent. So do I. You think I've been sitting here talking to you for fun? Because I might like you? Foolish."

A diversion.

Why?

"Hector, what have you done?"

THIRTEEN

Blair's arms cramped and burned from struggling and having her hands behind her back. There had to be a way out of here. She'd only been to Doc Drummond's house a couple of times, but she knew that Mitch Rydell's home was maybe ten minutes away by four-wheeler.

If she could get ahold of one of those, she might be able to mimic what Holt did the other night. She looked over to see Ronnie's head hanging to one side. Either he'd passed out or he was asleep. How could anyone sleep knowing death was coming for them?

"Ronnie...Ronnie!"

He lifted his head. "Leave me alone, Blair. Dawn left me anyway. This was all pointless." His voice rang with defeat.

"Don't give up yet, Ronnie. We've got to get out of here." He might have had a hand in everything, but he didn't deserve to be killed. Let the justice system dole out his punishment. "How many people are on the grounds?"

"Two or three stable hands. I've seen Sophia out here and her brother, Manny."

Sophia! If she could get to her, maybe she'd help them. But how often did the housekeeper come to the stables?

"Ronnie, after you won those other storage auctions, what did you do with the drugs?" If she could break the chair, she could slide the ropes off and free her legs. If she could run, she could handle having her hands bound. She rocked the chair back and forth, psyching herself up for the crash against the side of the stall.

"I brought them here."

"Why not have Keith bring them here from the trucking terminal? Why the storage unit?"

Blowing out a breath, Ronnie shifted. "I'm not sure, but Doc Drummond said that the DEA was watching closely. One agent had even been in town."

Could that have been the guy in the lake? Jeremy's friend?

"Keith rented a unit at the storage facility. He'd slip the merchandise to the manager, who would put it in a unit later. Keith would go to his personal storage space and take things out. Put things in. It looked legit. Then I'd come for the auction once a month. Nothing out of the ordinary there. And Keith wasn't part of that, so we couldn't be linked."

All the hands transferring drugs and money would keep law enforcement dazed and spinning their wheels. Sounded exactly like something Hector would do. Grief washed over her anew. Her brother was dead. Gone forever.

How would she tell Gigi and Dad? It was as if drugs dogged her at every turn.

Noises sounded outside the stable.

"Get her out! Move her. Take her to the cabin. We can't let him get to her. Not without finding where she's keeping the drugs."

Not Doc Drummond's voice. Female.

But she knew it well.

The stable door opened and Riella Drummond stood at the threshold. "Change of plans." She pulled out a gun as a wicked grin spread across her face. "However, you've been nothing but trouble to me, Ronnie. I told you to fix the mistake you made and you made things worse."

Pop!

Ears ringing, Blair jolted in the chair, gaping at the blood-spattered stable wall. Ronnie slumped over, one trickle of blood running down his brow. Her heart pounded and sweat slicked her back.

"Riella? You're working for that man who kidnapped me, too? You and Doc?"

Riella's eyes hardened. "You have it backward. He works for me. They all do. Now shut up!"

A string of pops reverberated like firecrackers on the Fourth of July. The sound of a car speeding came closer.

Riella's nostrils flared. Alejandro Gonzalez bustled inside, his face etched with worry. "Hector's here. His men took out the guards at the main house. We have to go. Now. Before he makes it out to the stables."

Hector!

"You saw him?" A flash of panic raced through Riella's eyes, and Alejandro's concern couldn't be missed. They were afraid of Hector. As they should be.

"No, just four of his men. But I'm not sure how many more they have, and he won't be far behind." He glared at Blair and raised his gun, aiming it at her head. "Looks like you get to keep your fingers."

Riella slapped his arm. "She comes with us. She's leverage and I want my product. Where is it, Blair?"

Blair's pulse hammered and her throat turned dry. "I— They're on my pond. The ducks. As decoys." Maybe she could buy herself some time. Send them on a wild-duck chase.

"Send Javier."

"Javier is dead," Doc Drummond said as he rushed toward them, laying a hand on Riella's shoulder. "We're holding them off, but we don't have much time. We've got to go. Kill her. Keep her. Your choice."

"You are supposed to help people, not poison them! How could you?" Blair screamed at Doc. He ignored her.

"Send someone to check out that pond. Now!" Riella ordered.

Doc Drummond nodded and ran.

"I'm getting Joseph out of here," Alejandro said. "If Hector finds him…"

Riella grabbed Blair's hair and jerked her head back, putting the gun under her chin. "Don't lie to me. Are those ducks on that pond?"

"I promise. The ducks are on the pond. Eleven of them. One was sold and someone stole it." Blair trembled; her teeth chattered while Riella cut the ropes at her feet. "You'll come with me. Ronnie got me back one kilo and that's why I killed him quickly. You, on the other hand, if you're lying…"

The sound of vehicles outside the stall had Riella's head snapping up. Sophia's brother, Manny, entered the stables. "Sophia's dead. He slit her throat. Hector slit her throat!" Pain flashed over his face. "I loved her." Venom filled his eyes. "And I'm going to kill Hector Salvador."

"Get a grip. He'll gut you like a pig before you ever think about making a move. Now go on, Joseph. Get in the car with your father. He's waiting."

"That's all you're going to say? She's your cousin and my fiancée!" Joseph howled.

Riella's eyes turned to slits. "People live and people die, Joseph. Which would you rather be?"

Manny was Joseph? Joseph was Alejandro's son? And Sophia wasn't his sister but…his fiancée?

Joseph glared at Riella, then stormed from the barn.

Blair's mind swirled with confusion.

Nothing made sense anymore. Except Holt. But where

was he? Did he even know she was in danger? *Please, God, show me mercy. Keep Holt safe.*

Shots were fired. Glass shattered. Someone must have hit a car window. Which meant... Hector was here!

Riella grabbed Blair and urged her forward toward the other side of the stables. "Run."

More gunfire ensued.

Hector was coming for her. Part of her rejoiced and part of her was scared out of her mind. Doubtful her safety was his chief concern. They ran down the length of the stables and stopped at the wall. Riella pointed her gun. "Sit."

Blair studied the gun. Riella would shoot her in the back if she ran. She did as she was told.

Riella pulled the handle of a rake. The wall opened. A secret door. "Get up. Get in. Now."

Blair scrambled to her feet and slipped inside the hidden room. Guns and piles of cellophane-wrapped money and drugs lined the walls. In the corner sat a glass tank filled with three snakes. Identical to the one from her bed. Riella opened a black briefcase and dug through it, taking a passport and a set of keys.

The woman motioned for her to sit down in the chair. She tied Blair's legs to it and grabbed a roll of duct tape, securing it across Blair's mouth.

Cursing, she marched to the hidden door and put her ear to it.

Someone yelled. Another pop sounded.

Then it was quiet. Eerily quiet. Riella cursed. "I should have ended Hector when I had the chance years ago." She tapped her finger to her lips. "I won't make that mistake again."

Blair listened. All she heard was her heart pummeling her ribs. She couldn't get a deep breath. The musty smell of hay and horses clogged her senses.

Riella lifted a rug from the floor and opened a small,

square wooden door. "Sit tight." She gave her a sickening smile. "I'll be back."

Blair wasn't sure where the door led or where Riella was going. Would Hector know about this secret room? How did Hector know she was here? Where was Holt? *God, please let him be okay. Let Gigi be okay.* Blair was going to die if she didn't break free. She needed one of those weapons.

If she could move her chair. She jerked and jumped until she had it turned toward the table. She worked on moving it backward. Sweat rolled down her face and spine. Her arms ached.

But she couldn't sit and do nothing. She'd escape. Run to town. Find Beckett.

Find Holt. If they hadn't gotten to him already.

Hunching from the weight of the chair attached to her body, she made it to the worktable. Groping around, she found her chance at escape. A knife! She worked it into her grasp, and then slowly, with little finesse, she started sawing the rope that secured her hands to the chair. At this rate, she'd never free herself, but she forged ahead.

Her hands trembled. Riella could come back at any time.

Another liar.

Right under her nose. Hidden among the hardworking, decent members of her town. A cold-blooded killer. And Doc Drummond, Sophia, Manny, too. Was anyone who they said they were? The rope thinned and she continued to saw.

She heard the sound of stall doors being kicked. Someone was hunting for her. She only hoped the lesser of the two evils found her, and right now that was Hector. Had to be. Anyone in the Juarez Cartel would know about the secret door.

If she could get the ropes off, she could rip the tape from her mouth and call to him.

Kicking continued outside. Someone was feeling along the wall, moving things. She strained to listen for a voice.

"I expected you sooner."

Hector! But who was he talking to?

"I got tied up."

Holt.

No! No. No. No. No. He was working with Hector?

"I take it you haven't found Blair yet," Holt said.

"No, but I know there's hidden rooms around here."

Blair heard continued knocking and groping against the wall. But she didn't want to be found. By Hector, Riella or Holt. Her insides crashed. Once again, she'd fallen for a liar. She'd finally given up her trust only to be betrayed again.

Tears stung the back of her eyes as she worked through the rope. It seemed pointless. She could barely move her hands.

"Everyone in the main house is dead," Holt said.

A murderer, too! That kiss, the way he protected and made her feel safe… How could he be a killer? A cold-blooded killer? How could Blair be so stupid?

"Good." Another tap. Another kick.

"Hector! Alejandro and Joseph got away," a new voice she didn't recognize hollered through the barn. "But Ricco and Tomas have intercepted them."

Hector roared, "Where are the Drummonds?"

"I'm not sure."

"Find Blair. She's behind one of these walls, I assure you. She won't be harmed until the drugs are found. Unless it gets down to the wire."

"Where are you going?" Holt demanded.

"I have business to attend to."

A few beats passed and Blair had no clue what was going on out there.

Hector laughed. "That's what I thought. See you soon, Holt."

Holt cursed and a huge boom sounded against the wall. Blair jumped, dropping her only weapon. She heard a scraping noise.

The door opened and Blair stared at Holt. The venom in his eyes turned to cool relief as he rushed to her and knelt. "Did she hurt you? Did anyone hurt you?" Holt touched her cheeks and she jerked away. Confusion dotted his expression.

"I'm going to take the duct tape off. I'll be gentle, but it's going to hurt. I'm sorry."

Sorry. He was *sorry*?

Holt removed the tape with a wince. Blair's skin stung, the removal leaving burning and rawness in its wake. "How could you?" She didn't want to cry. Tried not to. But tears came anyway. "You lied to me. You've been pretending this whole time."

Holt's eyes softened. Then he sighed as he cut her ropes free. "I wanted to tell you the truth, Blair. I did. But I couldn't. It's my job."

Working for a drug lord. "A job? And me? I'm a job?"

He touched her cheek and she slapped it away.

"At first. But when I knew you had nothing to do with Jeremy's disappearance—"

"What does Jeremy have to do with you working for Hector?"

Holt's eyes widened, then narrowed. "I don't work for Hector." He glanced behind the doors and must have realized she'd heard his conversation with her former brother-in-law. "Blair, honey, I'm the good guy. I'm undercover DEA. I'm looking for Jeremy."

The puzzle pieces clicked into place as confusion and hurt turned to unbridled rage. "Jeremy's dead! You killed him!"

Holt's hope and heart shattered into a million jagged pieces. Jeremy was dead? Grief. Shock. Helplessness ripped through him. He hadn't saved Trina. Was too late for Bryan. And now he'd failed Jeremy and Blair. No, Holt was no one's superhero.

"Ronnie Lawson's cousin murdered him because of *you*. How could you get him roped into such a dangerous situation! He's not a cop. He's a recovering addict!" Blair struck him across his cheek with such force it whipped his head in the opposite direction. He deserved it and then some.

"And then you used me! You *used* me!" she sobbed. "You knew my trust issues. You may not sell drugs, but you are...*not*...the good guy."

Holt swallowed the fiery knot in his throat and worked his jaw to try to gain some composure. She was right. One moment he believed God might be giving him a second chance, and now it was clear that Holt's dreams were once again dead in the water.

If he could only make her understand, but there wasn't time. The Drummonds were still on the loose. Hector had gone to butcher Alejandro and Joseph Gonzalez. Holt could have chased after him, but that would have left Blair vulnerable. Hector knew Holt would choose Blair.

The main house was a bloodbath, but it was empty. He needed to get in there and hopefully find a landline so he could call in Beckett. Hector's goons had laid a sneak attack on him while Hector distracted him. Knocked him out, giving Hector time to get here first. They'd taken his phone. His head still thrummed.

"I'm so sorry. I had to do my job. I had to protect you... I wanted to protect you... I love you, Blair. It's the truth."

"Don't you dare say that!"

It wasn't fair. But it might be the only opportunity to ever speak those words, and he wanted her to know.

Horses whinnied. "We have to get out of here. Now." Hopefully, Blair would be thinking straight enough to know she needed to go with him. "I won't hurt you. Let's go."

"Too late for that," she spat out, then pointed to the floor. "Riella used that door. I can only guess there's some kind of secret passageway. Don't know where it leads."

"Riella?" He lifted the trapdoor, and cool air and decay hit his face. "I thought Sophia was La Mujer," Holt murmured. His mind went in a million different directions.

"Sophia is dead." Blair pinched the bridge of her nose. "Riella is in charge of this nightmare."

Holt cupped the back of his neck and grimaced. "We need to climb down there. It's too risky going through the stable when we don't know where they are. My truck is at the main house. Let's get you to it and get you out of here." Once she was gone, he'd finish what he started. Hunt down the cartel members left standing and bring them to justice.

Blair hesitated, then wiped her damp cheeks with the back of her hand and climbed down into the underground tunnel that might have been used during the Prohibition to bootleg liquor. The dank, musty smell turned up Holt's nose.

"I think it leads to the main house," Holt said. Too dark to see much and he hadn't brought his penlight. Blair's footsteps shuffled behind him, but she remained silent. "Blair—"

"How could you have used my brother like that? Why did you do it?"

Holt's chest ached so much he couldn't breathe. "I didn't want him to get hurt, Blair. I cared about Jeremy. Saw potential in him that day I busted him during an undercover assignment and got him into rehab instead of arresting him."

The tunnel took a hard left.

"But then you put him out there as if he had training. Isn't that your job? To investigate, to go undercover, to *lie*?"

Her shaky voice stopped him in his tracks and he turned to face her in the dark. "I asked him to keep his ears open, not to sleuth. But he…he—"

"Felt obligated to you. Loyal. Like he owed you. And you used that."

Had he? "No. I never wanted him to get hurt."

She brushed past him. "All this time, I've been blaming myself and you let me. Let me worry. Was the private investigator even real? The information you supposedly got from him… Did it really come from you?"

"Yes," he murmured. "I wanted you to have some peace. To know we were on the case, Blair. That we were looking. You were afraid to go to the cops. I had to do something. I didn't want you to worry."

"How about tell the truth?" she hollered, her voice echoing. He didn't dare reprimand her.

"I wanted to," he whispered. "Especially when I knew I was falling in love with you. I even called my handler for permission after you were attacked in the woods." Sunlight cracked ahead. "But I had no choice. I had to follow orders. It's the job."

"So you did make a choice. You chose your job. Not me."

No, but he knew if he told her and she rejected him— hated him—he'd lose both. And he'd been right all along. Or had he? "Did you want me to choose you, Blair?"

He invaded her personal space to see her face.

"Doesn't matter now." A tremor threaded her weak voice.

She did love him. Or had. It had been in her kiss. Her eyes. The way she had surprised him with the sign on his window. The way she'd worried for him.

An ember of hope rose.

"I love you, Blair."

"Stop saying that! I don't believe you."

He grabbed her shoulder with his gun-free hand. "What do I gain by telling you that now? You do believe it. And I think you love me and it makes you mad. Because you're hurt. So am I. But it doesn't change the fact. I'm sorry for the lies. The secrets. For Jeremy. I am. But I'm not sorry for falling in love with you."

Blair held her hand up. "I can't. I can't deal with this right now."

Fine. This wasn't the time or the place, but they had to talk about it eventually.

"There's a door here. Stand back." Holt opened it. It led into the kitchen of the main house. Sophia lay dead on the floor. He listened. "I think it's clear." Holt cleared the kitchen. "Blair, come out. You need to get out of here."

She wouldn't come. Now was not the time to be stubborn. He'd messed up. Big-time. And she was dealing with the fact that her brother was dead. But she needed to keep moving. Holt would get her to safety and finish what he'd started. Now that he had a face to the head of the snake, he could crush it under his boot.

"Blair. Please, honey. We need to get you far away from this place."

Blair stepped out of the tunnel.

Riella Drummond behind her, gun to her head. "Too late."

FOURTEEN

Blair hadn't heard Riella come up behind her. The woman must have heard her yell at Holt and hid, waiting. The barrel of the gun bit into her cheek, but she held back a cry as she stumbled forward.

"Back up," Riella commanded.

Holt inched out of the kitchen and into the dining area of the house.

"I'm going to need you to put that gun down," Riella said as she kept Blair in front of her.

"Not a chance," Holt hissed.

"He's heroic," Riella said to Blair, her sweet perfume choking her. "I'll give him that."

Blair bit down on her lip and stared at the wall, her muscles watery and trembling. She couldn't look Holt in the eye.

She'd been nothing but a mark. A job. What could he gain by telling her he loved her?

Nothing.

But it didn't matter. Holt had a career that brought too much danger from the drug world into his life. Even if Jeremy hadn't been killed, Blair couldn't be a part of that world. Once again, her judgment had been clouded. And everything was falling apart.

"Riella," a man hollered.

"In the dining area."

Blair recognized one of the stable men. "Got the ducks. They were empty."

Riella growled and yanked Blair's hair until she nearly fell to her knees. She pointed the gun at Holt. "You tell me right now where they are or I kill him."

No! No more death. It had to stop. Her pulse spiked and her head swam.

"You get one shot. You that good? Because I am." Holt's cool tone shook Blair to the core.

A whizz like a bee sounded and the man next to Riella dropped to the floor, knocking over a dining chair.

"Hello, my sweet Blair." Hector entered from the north side with Doc Drummond in a headlock. The gun he'd used on Riella's stable hand was now jabbed against Doc's temple. "Gabriella Menendez. You are a vision. I can't believe you left me for this."

"What did you do to him, Hector?" Riella demanded. "Where's Alejandro and Joseph?"

Hector's smile said it all. They were dead. Doc Drummond's cheek was slicked with blood, a gaping gash down the middle of it. "I owed you one. Tit for tat. I like the red in your hair. Makes you look fiery and younger than forty. Did you throw a big party and not even invite me?"

Holt kept his gun on Riella, darting his eyes from Hector to Riella. Riella's gun was now gouging into the back of Blair's head.

A real Mexican standoff. Blair almost laughed out of delirium. "Hector, how did you find me?"

"Your darling and very beautiful sister called." He cocked his head, his voice husky and melodic. "Let her go. And I'll let the man you left me for live. Simple. Easy."

"Nothing is simple or easy with you." Riella gripped the gun. Blair bit back a moan.

"You're right, lover. It's not." He pulled the trigger.

Blair jolted and gasped.

Holt's nostrils flared.

Doc Drummond dropped to the floor, a small trickle of blood dribbling from the bullet hole in his forehead. Blair whimpered and shook. No one was going to get out of this alive.

Riella cursed in Spanish but kept her gun on Blair. Hector stood with a calm grin on his face, his gun aimed right on her. As if he'd done no more than swatted a fly.

Bad man, good man. It was still a life he'd taken.

God, help us.

Riella looked from Holt to Hector. "Why do you care if she lives or not?"

"She's *familia*. You know nothing of that kind of loyalty."

"You killed my husband. You think I'm going to let her walk out of here?" she screeched.

"The minute you put a bullet in her, I put one in you," Holt growled. "I *promise* you that."

"Ha!" Riella glared at Holt, but her eyes showed unease. She'd better believe him. Blair did. His eyes smoldered with deadly fury, but his body language was calm and cool. He didn't so much as flinch, but this was his life. Dangerous. Full of lies and games. Blair could never be a part of it. Never.

"You know I'm not lying," Holt said.

Riella glanced at Hector. "We can split the product. She has it hidden somewhere. We'll even give you a cut of the profit, hero-boy."

Hector's laugh was smooth and low, as if he'd heard a fabulous joke. "You don't know who he is, do you? Oh, this is rich."

"Who is he?" Riella stared intently at Holt. As if trying to recall if she should know him.

Hector snorted. "He's a Drug Enforcement agent. And not one for the taking."

Hearing it again sent tears into Blair's eyes. She was such an idiot. She should have picked up on it. The way he used a gun, searched her home, hot-wired ATVs! But she'd once again let her heart veil the truth.

"DEA," Riella huffed. Blair's back was about to break. She needed some relief. Could she ram Riella and hope for the best? No, it'd get her killed. If she could get her to aim her gun elsewhere, Holt could take a shot.

"Hector, we can kill him. Kill them both. Share the product." Riella's offer might tempt Hector. But Blair was banking on family loyalty prevailing. "She has it, you know? It was in the truck with her."

Hector's eyebrows rose and long lashes fluttered over eyes too gorgeous for a man to have, especially one so evil.

Riella tightened her grip on Blair's head, nails digging into her scalp.

Surely Hector wasn't considering it!

Holt kept his gun steady on Riella, as if assessing the situation or planning a sneak attack. But if he so much as moved, Blair would be dead.

Hector inhaled. "Blair, where's the cocaine?"

Lips trembling, she shook her head.

Hector made eye contact with Riella. They communicated silently, as only two people who knew each other well could.

"Blair, tell me where you've hidden it. This can all be over. I promised you freedom. I am a man of my word."

"I don't want to die, Hector," Blair cried.

"Tell me where it is…and you'll live."

Riella wouldn't let her live. And Blair wasn't so sure Hector would, either. She could trust no one.

Holt lurched forward and Hector trained his gun on

him. "I wouldn't. I said I wouldn't kill Blair. I never said I wouldn't kill you."

"Okay! Okay! I'll tell you." Blair was furious with Holt, but she would not watch him die.

Riella slammed the gun into Blair's cheekbone. "The truth this time." Turning to Hector she said, "Tell him to drop his gun. Show of good faith."

If Holt gave his gun up, either cartel leader could kill him. Then kill Blair. This couldn't be how it was going to end.

Hector huffed. "Holt, put the gun on the floor and kick it to me."

Holt kept his eyes trained on Hector as he slowly squatted to put his gun on the floor. Then he caught Blair's eye and mouthed, "I love you."

She closed her eyes as her lips quivered.

The gun clattered against the hardwood as Holt kicked it across the room. "Blair, no matter what happens to me, you can't give up the location of the drugs—"

"Shut up!" Riella hollered.

"Kids will die."

"She'll die if she doesn't tell us." Riella pointed the gun at Holt. "But you'll go first."

A gun fired.

Blair toppled to the floor as Riella crashed down on her. Hector brushed invisible lint from his shoulder. "It's all about trust, Blair. I give my word. I keep my word. You are *familia*. I needed the right moment to make my move." He picked Holt's gun up and pocketed it but trained his own gun on Holt. "In case you get any funny ideas."

Keeping an eye on Holt, he opened his hand for Blair to take. "Let's get you home safely."

Blair didn't know what to do. Would Hector kill Holt? She owed Hector now. "So you don't want the drugs?"

"No, I want the product. I have no plans to share them

with Riella, but she had every intention of taking you and this agent out."

"Hector, please don't make me tell you." Blair wiped her eyes. "Please."

"Where?"

Blair dipped her head. "I— They're…"

Hector crossed the room and put his gun to Holt's head. Still Holt's face remained resolute. "Do you wish for more death today, Blair?"

"Don't tell him, Blair. Please. I'm begging you."

"You'll die," she sobbed.

"And if you let that cocaine onto the street, many will die. You won't be able to live with yourself." His eyes pleaded with her. "I took this job for this very reason. Because I didn't care if I lived or died. Not after Trina. I knew the risks."

"How touching. Blair," Hector said. "Where?"

Even if he killed Holt, he'd end up killing Blair if she refused to give him the location. There was no way out of this. Blair darted her eyes from Hector to Holt. "And now? Do you want to live?"

Holt's intense blue eyes filled with moisture. "I want more for you to live. Guilt free."

Blair closed her eyes, then opened them and looked at Hector. "If I tell you, we both live?"

"You have my word," Hector said.

"And if I don't?"

"He dies."

"And what if I still won't tell you? You said you wouldn't kill me."

Hector sneered and she glimpsed the darkness inside him. "I said I wouldn't kill you. I never said I'd give you freedom."

He'd take her away. Lock her up somewhere. He'd wanted her in Dallas with him anyway. Maybe he'd let her go because he knew Riella had been here all along. Blair was an indirect line to her. But now that she was dead...

"And I never said anything about Gigi."

Blair's blood hammered in her temples. No. Not Gigi. She had to make a choice. One life. Or many lives.

God, I don't know what to do. Help me!

Everyone had risked something for her. Gigi had risked calling Hector. Holt had risked his life countless times. Didn't matter how hurt she was, she couldn't ignore the truth. Jeremy had sacrificed his own life to help others. To keep drugs off the streets because he knew how they sucked the life out of people.

Grandma Viola had made the sacrifice to leave her home, a place full of memories with Grandpa Henry, to come and raise her grandchildren after Mom had died. Even Hector, with his warped sense of loyalty and family, had taken a risk to come and rescue her. He could easily have been murdered by one of the Juarez Cartel members.

Too much bloodshed today. Too much anguish. Needless killing.

For what? Greed. Gain. Utter depravity. Selfish agendas.

"I've made my choice."

Holt braced himself. All his adult life he'd taken risks, some necessary and some careless. He'd stopped living. Talk about the walking dead. He'd been it. Until he came to Hope. To a town that had welcomed him with open arms. He never dreamed it would crack the hard layers covering his deceased heart. Never imagined that the one thing he wanted most would run off the road into a ditch and reveal that hope could still be found.

Living in the midst of a drug cartel, Blair had endured years of corruption and fear and she'd made it out. Not without some scars and a heavy dose of paranoia. But she'd fought for a better life, for a dream, and she protected the people she loved in a way that made him crave it, too. Not the feeling of being protected, but being loved by Blair.

Here he was. The moment of truth. He was ready to go.

God, I've wasted a lot of years. I've been angry and cold for so long. And yet You still have worked on my behalf to bring me healing, even when I didn't realize I needed it. I want to live, but I want Blair to live more. So give her the strength and the courage to do what's right. To do what's best. Help her make a wise decision. I'm okay with coming home if You're ready for me.

Holt held back his emotion for fear that Blair would misinterpret it as fear of dying. He wasn't afraid. Trina hadn't been, either. In those last moments, he'd held her hand and prayed with everything in him for healing, but she'd whispered Holt's name.

It's okay, Holt. It...it doesn't hurt anymore. I love you.

He'd told her he loved her, too, but he'd still hurt. Even as she closed her eyes and took one last gasp for air, he'd ached all over until he couldn't breathe. He'd stopped breathing after that.

Until Blair.

"So, what is your choice?" Hector waited. Patiently.

Blair held Holt's gaze. A shudder ripped down his back. The resolve in her eyes frightened him. "Blair..." he rasped.

"You let Holt and Gigi live. And I'll go with you. A prisoner...whatever," she choked out. "Because I can't give you those drugs, Hector. I can't let more people die. Not today. Not with that poison. So I'll go willingly. But you have to promise that if I do, Gigi and Holt will never be harmed. I know you're a man of your word."

"No!" Holt lunged for her, but Hector clipped his jaw with his gun. A searing pain tore through his body.

"Fine. I will grant their lives for yours. You'll like living under my protection. Who knows, Blair, you may even grow to care for me. In time."

He turned to Holt and pointed to the dining room chair. "Sit. I can't have you attempting something heroic and stupid. I've promised our girl your life. Blair, on your stomach, facedown, hands out. I don't want you getting any wild ideas while I tie him up."

Blair eased onto the floor. "Just don't hurt him, Hector. Please. Or Gigi. I'll do whatever and go wherever you want."

Sirens whirred in the distance.

Hector raised his head toward the window, giving Holt a cracked window of opportunity. He rammed him in the side, knocking Hector off balance, and grabbed the gun, twisting Hector's wrist.

Hector released the gun and fell to the floor. Holt fell on top of him.

The gun fired.

Blair screeched.

The door burst open and Beckett flew inside. "Holt! You hurt?" He slid to his knees and touched Holt's chest, then raised a bloody hand. "Oh, Holt," he whispered.

Holt released a heavy breath. "It's…it's not mine, man. It's not mine."

Beckett let out a relieved sigh, then checked Hector's vitals. "He's alive, but barely. He's going to wish he had died once he's behind bars."

Blair hovered in the corner, knees drawn up, head resting in her hands and shoulders shaking. Holt pulled himself up and crawled to her. Like he had the night he saved her from the snake. He touched her shoulders to coax her into his lap, but she wrenched away. "Don't touch me," she murmured. "I can't… Just…"

But she'd risked her life for his. How could she reject him now?

Holt let the slicing pain slide away and he mustered the strength to put distance between them, when all he desired was to be close to her. To make the hurt disappear. The hurt he'd inflicted.

Paramedics arrived and Beckett motioned them to Blair. He laid a hand on Holt's shoulder and leaned in. "She's in shock. That's all," he whispered, and gave a brotherly squeeze.

No. She was done with Holt. Tired of death. Afraid Gigi might have been hurt. Jeremy was dead. And Holt couldn't erase his part. Couldn't erase Jeremy's death. Couldn't erase the deception or lies.

The paramedics put a blanket around Blair and helped her to the ambulance.

Holt stood in the Drummonds' driveway. Death and blood everywhere. No one from the Juarez Cartel had been spared.

Pain coursed through every vein in Holt's body and yet within the cavern of dark pain, a light, warm and encompassing, shone. It hovered on the edges and grew, eating away the darkness, the emptiness, the hollow areas. Eating away the heavy veil that hid salvation until nothing was left but hope. And faith. And love.

"We did a search over at the Lawson place. We found an area about a mile off the property. Looked like it'd been unearthed. Took a chance. We…we found Jeremy Sullivan. He's gone to autopsy. But we'll need identification to be certain."

Holt squeezed his eyes shut. Jeremy hadn't deserved evil for the good he was trying to do. Holt didn't understand it. Didn't have a single answer as to why Jeremy was taken. Just like he never had a single answer for why

Trina died. But he had hope. Hope for healing. Hope for change. "I'll do it."

"You sure?" Beckett asked.

"Yeah. Blair's been through enough and I don't want her to remember him this way. I'll…I'll do it." It was his responsibility anyway.

"I can give you a ride." Beckett walked to his SUV.

"How'd you know we were here?"

"One of Mitch Rydell's stable hands said they heard multiple gunshots fired over here. Doc Drummond has done a lot of medical work in South America. Didn't really click earlier. Guess I didn't want it to. But I had a hunch."

"I'm glad you did."

"So, what's next for you? You think you'll settle down here? I could always use a good deputy." He winked. "Or a name next to mine on the ballot for sheriff. I'd win being homegrown here, but you'd give me a good run for my money."

Holt chuckled but it hurt to do so. He hurt absolutely everywhere. "I need to report in, get the DEA down here. There'll be lots of paperwork. I may never shovel my way out of it. Worst part of the job."

Beckett nodded and handed him a bottle of water from the drink holder. "Let's say you do. Shovel your way out."

Could he come back to this town without Blair in his life the way he wanted her to be? Could she handle seeing him every day right next door? There was a lot to consider. As much as he loved it here, could he leave Memphis? The DEA?

He had a lot of catching up to do with God. A lot of praying for direction. He'd been called to come forth like Lazarus. But he still needed some time to unbind the grave clothes. To strip away what was left of his hopeless, faithless life and raw emotions. Time to step out of the tomb into the light. And more than anything, he needed to hang out with the One who'd resurrected him.

FIFTEEN

The week following the nightmare at Doc and Riella Drummond's house had been long and hard. Blair had spent most of her days being strong for Gigi and Dad. Nights had been spent curled up in bed crying and sinking into the pages of her Bible. The only way she could find any peace to sleep.

She'd been lied to. Deceived.

Her heart had been stolen and smashed.

She'd never hug her brother again.

The shop had been closed. Partly because she had so much to work through. She'd been interviewed by Beckett—and as gracious as he'd been, he couldn't keep her past or what had transpired from the town. She'd gone into Memphis to give her interview with the DEA. Holt hadn't been around. She'd spoken with an Agent Greg Carson. Told him she'd hidden the drugs in the gift boxes under the tree in her window display, and they'd recovered it all, including the kilo stolen from Hunter's house.

Part of her was relieved not to see Holt. The other part wanted to see those wildly blue eyes, touch that shaggy black hair and trace a finger around the cleft in his chin.

Jeremy's funeral had been excruciating but he hadn't died in a crack house, homeless, jobless and addicted to drugs. He'd died a hero. Working to put away evil men with murderous agendas. She found peace in that. And while she'd love to continue blaming Holt for Jeremy's death, she couldn't.

Holt had been doing his job. And now as Blair looked back on all the things that Jeremy said about his mystery friend, she couldn't believe she'd missed that it was Holt. His friend was brave, stubborn, intense at times. Had always been loyal to him and done whatever he could to protect him, even if it meant speaking the truth out of love. If ever there was someone he needed to count on, it was the mystery friend.

She owed Holt, in a sense, for pulling her brother from the ashes. Doing what she'd tried and failed to do so many times. Holt hadn't sent Jeremy snooping, even if he'd asked him to keep his eyes and ears open. Jeremy chose to do that all by himself.

Choices had to be made every day. Right or wrong. Consequences or not. Choosing was better than doing nothing. Which was what Blair had been doing. Living in limbo. Running like a hamster on a wheel simply because she feared making the wrong choice.

Even when she prayed, she didn't always make the right decisions. But she'd learned from her mistakes and God had been with her, even when she'd totally bombed out. When she turned left instead of going right. When she ignored the gnawing in her gut, like when she chose to marry Mateo.

What was the answer for her and Holt? Was there one?

Holt's career was all about taking life-threatening risks. Long hours. Long nights spent away and undercover where he couldn't call or check in. Blair might go crazy. She simply couldn't handle being with that kind of man. Was that selfish of her?

Someone had to fight for justice, take risks, save lives.

Was it fair to penalize Holt for being a hero? For trying to make the world a better place?

Blair needed to get out. Get some air. She had been hiding in her house too long. At first, out of fear that people would judge her and try to run her out of town.

But the people in her community hadn't. Her fridge was proof people loved her. Food for decades had poured in. That must be what forgiveness really looked like. Unconditional love and grace in the form of a potluck and a tableful of mercy. Chocolate and pecan pie kind of mercy.

She walked the cobbled streets, waved to friends. Welcomed the July heat. Tonight was the Fireworks on the Square. An amazing display of beauty in the sky set to the tune of songs about country and freedom. Songs about those who risked their lives to fight for justice.

Someone had to do it. Someone like Holt.

She stopped in the square. Took in the red, white and blue bows and banners that hung around the gazebo and the makeshift stage where Mayor Tuesday would give her annual freedom speech. The woman had a way with words. Not a dry eye in town would be had tonight.

"Hello, Blair."

Blair turned to see Aurora Daniels in her business suit, with her shiny strawberry blond hair and twinkling blue eyes. Not a drop of sweat on her brow. How was that possible?

"Hey, Aurora. How's court?"

"Judge Treadwell is a grouch. But I'm winning. So it's a good day." She sipped her coffee.

"How do you do it? Defend people like the Drummonds? Like Hector Salvador?"

"Everyone deserves a fair trial."

"Have you ever defended people like those in the cartels?"

Aurora's pointed but perfect nose twitched. "Everyone in the cartel is dead. I don't defend the dead."

But she hadn't answered her question. And she'd been beyond interested in the DEA agent at the bottom of the lake.

"You coming tonight? To the fireworks?" Blair asked.

"Maybe. I have a lot to do."

"With all the criminals in Hope?" Blair smirked.

Aurora raised her cup. "Take care, Blair. I'm very sorry about what happened to your brother." Genuine sympathy poured from Aurora's wintry blue eyes.

"Thank you."

"I don't cook much, but if you need coffee, it's on the house. Anytime."

Blair nodded and watched as Aurora strode down the sidewalk, heels clicking. Beckett drove by, waved to Blair, then slowed next to Aurora and rolled down his passenger window. Blair couldn't be sure what he said, but by the way Aurora bristled and scowled it hadn't been anything pleasant. But then Aurora tried to set free the very people Beckett arrested.

Laughter rang through the throng of people gathered downtown, and families broke out lawn chairs, blankets and picnic baskets, sharing desserts and settling in for the live music that preceded the speech and fireworks display.

Gigi and Hunter sat under a maple tree. Her new ring glittered in the sunlight.

They were on again. Till death do them part. Blair was happy for G, even if Blair had given her grief for calling Hector. But as Gigi put it, someone had to do something. And it wasn't going to be Blair.

That had been true. She paused and turned the knob to Holt's fake store and slipped inside. Nothing had been removed. Today would have been opening day.

Blair switched the white lights on in the window display. Tears burned and a lump formed in her throat as she thought of what would never be.

Finally, Holt had tunneled his way out of paperwork. Read over Blair's interview. Missed her and the people of Hope every day. He'd opted out of Jeremy's funeral. Blair needed time to grieve and say goodbye without Holt reminding her of everything bad that had happened. He'd made his way to Jeremy's grave after the service. Said his goodbyes. Had a few tearful laughs as he reminisced with the memory of his old friend.

He'd thought about what Beckett had said. Even had lunch with him a few times over the past couple of weeks. In Memphis. Blair needed space.

So had Holt. He'd been immersed in the Word and had been going to church again. It felt good. Right. He'd been praying about direction. Was working with the DEA God's plan? Yeah. Even though Holt hadn't meant for it to be. He'd been part of helping people, like Jeremy. And it had brought him here.

To Hope.

He stood at the back door of The Great Outdoors. His store. Leased in his name now...if Blair was okay with that. He wouldn't stick around if she told him to go. But he hoped—because he was hoping again—that she'd tell him to stay. Being in the DEA had brought him to her.

And there was no denying she'd been divinely ordained in his life. The whole rocky journey had been part of God's plan.

But now? Did he want to be a sheriff? A sheriff's deputy?

No. No, he didn't.

God hadn't just resurrected his faith.

He'd resurrected his dream.

Holt opened the back door and tiptoed inside. The

lights twinkled from the window display up front. The sun had gone down and the music blared from the square. He loved this place.

Blair stood in front of the display. Her hand trailing down the side of the pup tent.

"That tent over there?" Holt murmured. Blair started but didn't turn around. Not the best sign. "That tent housed a couple on their wedding night. They had an outdoor ceremony near a pond. A pasture with horses grazing in the background. Floating candles flickering on the green water. That night, they held each other and gazed up at the stars dreaming together. Making plans. And then they made the best, most tender memories inside that tent."

Blair dropped her hand from the tent. Holt moved closer to her, his hiking boots clunking across the wood. She loved the pretend game. Would she play along? See that it wasn't so much pretend as it was his hope for the future. New memories. With her. And only her.

She raised her hand and swiped her eyes. He wanted to wipe her tears, hated that he'd caused them. Finally, she turned, so beautiful, so amazing, knocking him breathless. "And did they have a happily-ever-after?"

Holt had been contemplating that. The whole happily-ever-after and how much Blair thought she wanted it. "No."

Blair's eyes widened and her eyebrows lifted.

"They didn't." He closed the distance and stroked her cheek with his thumb. "Because life is full of bumps in the road. Ups and downs. Disappointments. Failures. And pain. Pain that sometimes feels like it's slaying us. Life isn't always happy. So they didn't get a happily-ever-after. Instead—" he glanced at her signage, the bell that gave an angel its wings with each ring "—they got a wonderful life. For better. And for worse. They were together."

Her lip quivered. "I'm so sorry. For what I said about your part in Jeremy's death. I didn't really mean that."

"Thank you," he whispered, searching her eyes for hope. For answers he desperately wanted.

"And I know why you lied. It was your job and you were trying to protect me. I did the same thing for Gigi. I withheld information because I loved her."

Holt slowly nodded and grinned, his heart ballooning with promise. "So you know."

Blair sniffed and touched his cheek. "I know. You love me."

"I love you," he echoed.

"I've made so many wrong choices I was afraid to make any choices."

He framed her face. "Until you made the choice to become some kind of slave to Hector. You crazy, crazy woman. Did you think I could ever live knowing you had done that? I'd have come for you. You know that, don't you?"

"I would have hoped so."

He traced her lips with his finger.

She shivered. "I'm ready to live again. To stop being afraid to make choices concerning my life."

"Good." He inched toward her lips. "Because I have a question that will require a choice. But I'll make it easy for you."

She giggled, gasping as his lips grazed hers. Oh, he hoped he always had that effect on her.

"Blair Sullivan, will you marry me? A, yes." He pecked her on the lips. "B, yes." He kissed an eyelid. "C, yes." Pressed another to her other eyelid. "D, all of the above." Hovering over her mouth, he waited, heart galloping.

She opened her eyes. "You do make choices easy."

"They won't always be, Blair. I'm stubborn. Set in my ways. And you're opinionated and sassy—which I adore."

Blair beamed. "I love you, Holt…" Her jaw dropped. "I just realized something."

"What?"

"I don't know your name. Your real name! I'm about to say *yes* to a stranger!"

He grabbed her up and placed a hard smack on her lips. "You said *yes*!" Everything was right in his world.

"I said I was *going* to say *yes*. I want to know what my last name is going to be."

He laughed. "I want you to become Mrs. Holt McKnight."

Blair's eyes sparkled. "Blair McKnight. I love it."

"I love it more. And I'm moving here. Bought the store. I want the life I pretended to have."

Blair's eyes leaked tears. "I was coming to Memphis. To tell you I'm okay being with an agent. With a real superhero."

He tucked a strand of hair behind her ear. "I love that you'd be okay with that. I do. But I want this. This life in Hope. With you. I like being next door to you at work, and in the same house with you at night."

Blair wrapped her arms around his neck. "I love you, Holt McKnight."

"And I love you." He sank into the kiss then. No need for Fireworks on the Square. They were creating a celebration of their own. Freedom. Joy. Hope. Faith.

All sealed with one glorious kiss.

EPILOGUE

Blair shivered as she entered the store, the bell ringing above. An angel got its wings. She giggled and switched on the lights, then dashed to the back of the store and grabbed her early Christmas present for Holt.

It was the day before Christmas Eve and she had to hurry before heading over for Christmas in the Square. They were showing *It's a Wonderful Life* and serving hot chocolate and cookies.

The door opened and the bell jingled. Then it jingled again. And again. Frowning, she entered the room and the sight of Holt sent warm fuzzies through her. Her husband since October. They'd had an outdoor wedding. A honeymoon under the stars but not in a pup tent. A great big white tent with a queen-size bed and flowers all around. It had been blissful.

He stood laughing. His hair poking out from under his black knit cap, a Christmas scarf wrapped around his neck and tucked into his gray goose-down coat. A sight to behold. And all hers.

"Why are you doing that? Stop opening and closing the door." She laughed and frowned.

"It's almost Christmas Eve. I think a whole host of angels need wings." He shut the door and snorted. "I would have closed up earlier, but that new girl who took over the

Magnolia Inn came in and bought a canoe. In December. Weird, huh? But then, she's from Ireland."

"And what? They canoe in December?" Mrs. McKay died last month and willed the Magnolia Inn to her two great-granddaughters, Claire and Keely McKay. Blair loved their accents.

"I don't know if they canoe or not, but we should take a trip to Ireland sometime." Holt drew Blair into his arms.

"We should. But first, I have a gift for you. An early Christmas present."

Holt raised an eyebrow, then stole a kiss on her neck. "Do you, now?"

She giggled and pushed away from him. God had been so good to her. Blessed her in good times and in the rough ones.

"Okay. I'm ready. Do I have to close my eyes?"

"No." She handed him the small silver-wrapped gift box.

He smirked. "It's not cocaine, is it? Dead rat?"

She gave him a pointed look.

He chuckled and tore into the paper, then ripped the lid off the box. Like a little kid. His eyes grew as big as the Grinch's heart. Three sizes! His mouth fell open. "It's a plus sign."

"Merry Christmas, Daddy."

He dropped the test on the counter and wrapped her in a bear hug. "I love you so much."

"I love you, too. And if he's a boy, I'd like to name him Jeremy Renard McKnight. A piece of him and a piece of you…in a way."

Holt chuckled into her neck and kissed her on the tender spot below her ear. "No George Bailey?"

She pulled back, full of joy, full of expectant hope. How she adored this man who'd slipped into her town and her heart undercover. "Maybe they'll be twins."

"Bite your tongue, woman." But the sparkle in his blues revealed his hope for exactly that.

She fell headlong into the warmth and sweetness of his kiss. There was no denying it:

This was a wonderful life.

* * * * *

If you liked this story from Jessica R. Patch,
check out her other Love Inspired Suspense titles:

FATAL REUNION
PROTECTIVE DUTY

Available now from Love Inspired!

Find more great reads at www.LoveInspired.com

Dear Reader,

I hope you enjoyed Holt and Blair's story. Maybe you can relate to Holt. He had big dreams and lots of plans that he'd committed to the Lord, but a tragedy in his life ripped them out of his grasp and he feared to dream again. To hope again. He buried his faith when he buried someone he loved deeply. One of my favorite accounts in the Bible is Jesus traveling to raise Lazarus from the dead. Lazarus's sisters were devastated. All seemed lost. No hope. And yet Jesus called Lazarus to come forth. The passage tells us that he immediately arose and came out of the tomb, still bandaged from his grave clothes.

Maybe all your hopes and dreams have decayed in a tomb built by tragedy, pain, loss. If you can muster up even a mustard-seed-sized amount of faith to believe that God can heal your heart, raise up dead or new dreams—like Holt, you'll find that peace and joy you've been craving for so long but were afraid to grab hold of. Maybe it's time for you to trust Jesus to say, "Come forth!" and see what He raises to life!

I'd love for you to get *Patched In*! My newsletter subscribers receive first looks at book covers, excerpts and occasional FREE novellas, as well as notifications when new books release. Sign up today at *www.jessicarpatch.com*. Please feel free to email me at *jessica@jessicarpatch.com*, join me on my Facebook page, *www.Facebook.com/jessica rpatch*, for daily discussions and take a peek at my Pinterest board to meet the characters and get an up-close view of the scenes from the book.

Warmly,
Jessica

REQUEST YOUR FREE BOOKS!

2 FREE INSPIRATIONAL NOVELS
PLUS 2
FREE
MYSTERY GIFTS

Love Inspired®

YES! Please send me 2 FREE Love Inspired® novels and my 2 FREE mystery gifts (gifts are worth about $10). After receiving them, if I don't wish to receive any more books, I can return the shipping statement marked "cancel." If I don't cancel, I will receive 6 brand-new novels every month and be billed just $4.99 per book in the U.S. or $5.49 per book in Canada. That's a saving of at least 17% off the cover price. It's quite a bargain! Shipping and handling is just 50¢ per book in the U.S. and 75¢ per book in Canada.* I understand that accepting the 2 free books and gifts places me under no obligation to buy anything. I can always return a shipment and cancel at any time. Even if I never buy another book, the two free books and gifts are mine to keep forever.

105/305 IDN GH5P

Name	(PLEASE PRINT)

Address	Apt. #

City	State/Prov.	Zip/Postal Code

Signature (if under 18, a parent or guardian must sign)

Mail to the **Reader Service:**
IN U.S.A.: P.O. Box 1867, Buffalo, NY 14240-1867
IN CANADA: P.O. Box 609, Fort Erie, Ontario L2A 5X3

**Are you a subscriber to Love Inspired® books
and want to receive the larger-print edition?
Call 1-800-873-8635 or visit www.ReaderService.com.**

* Terms and prices subject to change without notice. Prices do not include applicable taxes. Sales tax applicable in N.Y. Canadian residents will be charged applicable taxes. Offer not valid in Quebec. This offer is limited to one order per household. Not valid for current subscribers to Love Inspired books. All orders subject to credit approval. Credit or debit balances in a customer's account(s) may be offset by any other outstanding balance owed by or to the customer. Please allow 4 to 6 weeks for delivery. Offer available while quantities last.

Your Privacy—The Reader Service is committed to protecting your privacy. Our Privacy Policy is available online at www.ReaderService.com or upon request from the Reader Service.

We make a portion of our mailing list available to reputable third parties that offer products we believe may interest you. If you prefer that we not exchange your name with third parties, or if you wish to clarify or modify your communication preferences, please visit us at www.ReaderService.com/consumerchoice or write to us at Reader Service Preference Service, P.O. Box 9062, Buffalo, NY 14240-9062. Include your complete name and address.

LI15

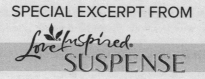
"I looked up the license plate of the black sedan from the restaurant," Miles said, his expression grim. "The sedan is registered to Sci-Tech."

"They sent gunmen after us?" Paige asked in a strained whisper.

"Yeah, that's what it looks like."

"They're after me because of my ex-husband, aren't they?"

"I think so, yes." Miles reached over and cradled her icy hands in his. "I'm sorry."

Paige gripped his hands tightly. "You have to find Travis before it's too late."

He didn't want to point out that it might already be too late. Whatever Abby had seen on the tablet had frightened her to the point she wouldn't speak. Had Travis told her to keep quiet? Or had she seen something horrible? He found himself hoping for the first option, but feared the latter.

"I'm not sure where to look for Travis," he admitted. "There's no way to know where he'd go to hide if he thought he was in danger."

"Did you give the police the list of names I gave you?" Paige asked. "I know they're only a few names, but…"

"I've been searching on their names, but I haven't found anything yet. At least we have another link to Sci-Tech. No wonder they were stonewalling me."

"I might be able to get inside the building," Paige offered.

"No." His knee-jerk reaction surprised him, and he tried to backpedal. "I mean, if they're the ones behind this, then it's not safe for you to go there. Besides, how would you get in?"

She lifted her uncertain gaze to his. "I know a couple of the security guards pretty well. If I waited until after-hours, when there's only one security guard manning the desk, I might be able to convince them to let me in."

"I know you want to help, but it's not worth the risk." He couldn't stand the idea of Paige walking into the equivalent of the lion's den. "You don't know for sure which security guard would be on duty. And besides, if anything happened—Abby would be lost without you."

She blinked, and he thought he saw the glint of tears. "Logically, I know you're right, but it's hard to sit back and do nothing, not even trying."

"I'll find a way to do something while keeping you and Abby safe." He couldn't stand the thought of her worrying about things she couldn't change. He'd protect her, no matter what.

Don't miss
THE ONLY WITNESS
by Laura Scott, available February 2017 wherever
Love Inspired® Suspense books and ebooks are sold.

www.LoveInspired.com

LISEXP0117

Wyatt glanced at Carolina, but she wouldn't meet his
eyes.

Was she feeling guilty over all Matty's firsts that she'd
denied Wyatt? First breath, first word, the first step Matty
took?

He couldn't say he felt sorry for her. She should be
feeling guilty. She'd made the decision to walk away.
She'd created these consequences for herself, and for
Wyatt, and most of all, for Matty.

But today wasn't a day for anger. Today was about
spending time with his son.

"What do you say, little man?" he asked, scooping
Matty into his arms and leading Carolina to his truck.
"Do you want to play ball?"

Not knowing what Matty would like, he'd pretty
much loaded up every kind of sports ball imaginable—a
football, a baseball, a soccer ball and a basketball.

Carolina flashed him half a smile and shrugged
apologetically. "I'm afraid I don't know much about

these games beyond being able to identify which ball goes with which sport."

"That's what Matty's got a dad for."

He didn't really think about what he was saying until the words had already left his lips.

Their gazes met and locked. She was silently challenging him, but he didn't know about what. Still, he kept his gaze firmly on hers. His words might not have been premeditated, but that didn't make them any less true. He was sorry if he'd hurt her feelings, though. He wanted to keep things friendly between them.

"There's plenty of room on the green for three. What do you say? Do you want to play soccer with us?"

Shock registered in her face, but it was no more than what he was feeling. This was all so new. Untested waters.

Somehow, they had to work things out, but kicking a ball around together at the park?

Why, that almost felt as if they were a family.

And although in a sense that was technically true, Wyatt didn't even want to go down that road.

He had every intention of being the best father he could to Matty. And in so doing, he would establish some sort of a working relationship with Carolina, some way they could both be comfortable without it getting awkward. He just couldn't bring himself to think about that right now.

Or maybe he just didn't want to.

Don't miss
THE DOCTOR'S TEXAS BABY
by Deb Kastner, available February 2017
wherever Love Inspired® books and ebooks are sold.

www.LoveInspired.com